STORIES OF TAILS AND WHISKERS

Look out for all of these enchanting story collections

by Enid Blyton®

Animal Stories
Cherry Tree Farm
Christmas Stories
Christmas Tales
Christmas Treats
Christmas Wishes
Fireworks in Fairyland
Five-Minute Stories
Magical Fairy Tales
Mr Galliano's Circus
Nature Stories
Pet Stories
Rainy Day Stories
Springtime Stories
Stories for Bedtime
Stories of Magic and Mischief
Stories of Mischief Makers
Stories of Rotten Rascals
Stories of Spells and Enchantments
Stories of Tails and Whiskers
Stories of Wizards and Witches
Stories of Wonders and Wishes
Summer Adventure Stories
Summer Holiday Stories
Summertime Stories
Tales of Tricks and Treats
The Wizard's Umbrella
Winter Stories

Enid Blyton

STORIES OF TAILS AND WHISKERS

Illustrations by Mark Beech

HODDER

HODDER CHILDREN'S BOOKS

This collection first published in Great Britain in 2023
by Hodder & Stoughton

3 5 7 9 10 8 6 4 2

A CIP catalogue record for this book is available from the British Library.

ISBN 978 1 444 96924 5

Typeset by Avon DataSet Ltd, Alcester, Warwickshire

Printed and bound in India by Manipal Technologies Limited

The paper and board used in this book are made from
wood from responsible sources.

MIX
Paper from
responsible sources
FSC
www.fsc.org
FSC™ C104740

Hodder Children's Books
An imprint of Hachette Children's Group
Part of Hodder & Stoughton Limited
Carmelite House
50 Victoria Embankment
London EC4Y 0DZ

An Hachette UK Company
www.hachette.co.uk
www.hachettechildrens.co.uk

Contents

The Dog with the Very Long Tail

The Dog with the Very Long Tail

THERE WAS once a dog with a very long tail. His name was Ginger, because he was just the colour of ginger, and he belonged to little Terry Brown.

Terry was fond of Ginger. He went about everywhere with his dog, and played games with him when he came out of school. Ginger loved Terry too, and would have done anything in the world for him. His tail never stopped wagging when he was with Terry.

One day Terry was very excited. There was to be a grand garden party in the Rectory garden, with sweet stalls, competitions, baby shows and dog shows. Terry was going, and he made up his mind to buy some peppermint sweets and to have a bottle of ginger beer and two dips in the bran-tub.

'There's to be a maypole dance too,' he told his mother, 'and I shall watch that. Mr Jones is having a coconut shy, and I shall have two tries at that.'

'Well, I will give you half a crown to spend,' said his mother. 'That should be plenty for everything, Terry.'

'Oh, thank you,' said Terry. 'I shall take Ginger with me and buy him a treat. He'll love that.'

When the day came Terry and Ginger walked to the garden party. Terry had the half-crown coin in his pocket, and he was planning all he would do with it. He looked round the grounds and decided that he would start with a go at the coconut shy. He thought it would be lovely to win a big nut.

'I'll have a go,' he said to the man. 'How much?'

'Three balls for sixpence,' said the man. Terry put his hand into his pocket to get his money – and, oh, dear me – it was gone! There was a hole at the bottom and the coin had dropped out!

Terry was so upset. He went back to look for his money but he couldn't find it anywhere. Ginger went with him and was just as upset as his master.

'Now I can't buy any sweets or ginger beer, or have any dips in the bran-tub,' said poor Terry sadly. 'All my money is gone. Oh, Ginger, I do think it's bad luck, don't you?'

Ginger pushed his nose into Terry's hand and looked up at him with big brown eyes. He was very sorry for his master. He thought he would go and look for the lost money by himself, so he trotted off, nose to ground, trying to find the coin.

Suddenly Ginger came to where a great many dogs were all gathered together with their masters and mistresses, and he ran up to a collie dog called Rover, a great friend of his.

'What are you all doing here?' he asked Rover.

'Waiting for the dog shows,' answered Rover.

'I hope you win a prize,' said Ginger.

'Aren't you going in for the show?' asked Rover.

'No,' said Ginger, wagging his tail. 'My little master, Terry, is very sad. He has just lost all his money and I'm looking for it.'

Just at that moment the dog show began, and the dogs moved into the ring. Ginger stayed to watch. It was a comic dog show, and there were prizes for the hairiest dog, the noisiest dog, the dog with the saddest eyes and the dog with the shortest legs. Ginger thought it was very funny.

'Now then!' cried the man who was running the dog show. 'Which dog has the longest tail! Come along, everybody! I've got a measuring tape here to measure the tails with! Bring in your dogs! The one with the longest tail gets half a crown!'

Now when Ginger heard that, a good idea suddenly came into his head! Surely no dog had a longer tail than his! Everybody laughed at his tail because it was so very long. He would trot into the ring and show it to the judge!

So Ginger pushed his way through the people watching and trotted into the ring, where other dogs stood having their tails measured.

Ginger went right up to the judge and stuck his tail out to be measured.

'Ha!' cried the judge. 'Here is a dog who thinks his tail is quite the longest! Stand still then, and let me measure it!'

All the people laughed and Ginger stood quite still while the judge measured his tail.

'My goodness, what a long one!' he cried. 'Why, it's a foot and a half long! Little dog, I think you must have the prize! Who is the owner of this dog? Will he please step forward and take the prize?'

Now, Terry happened to be peeping at the dog show at that moment and was most astonished to see his dog. He was still more surprised to hear that Ginger had won a prize, and he stepped into the ring to take it for him.

'Half a crown!' said the judge, and he gave a nice bright coin to Terry. Then he patted Ginger, and the grateful dog licked his hand.

'Good old Ginger!' said Terry, running off with him. 'Fancy you thinking of putting yourself in for the longest-tailed dog! I know why you did it, Ginger! You did it because you were sorry that I had lost my money! You're the cleverest, dearest dog in the world, and I'm going to buy you a whole bag of treats!'

Ginger wagged his long tail and barked for joy. He bounded along by Terry and when his little master had bought him all that he had said he would, he wagged his long tail two hundred times a minute.

'Wuff, wuff!' he said, and he ate up the biscuits in one gulp!

'Good old Ginger,' said Terry. 'Now come along to the coconut shy! I'll see if I can't get a coconut this time!'

Off they went – and Terry knocked down the largest coconut of the lot! Wasn't he lucky? Then he went to buy some sweets and some ginger beer, and had three dips in the bran-tub – all with Ginger's prize money; and you may be sure there wasn't a prouder dog than Ginger at the garden party that day!

The Gentle Scarecrow

The Gentle Scarecrow

ONCE UPON a time there were two small robins. They had met one early spring morning in the old hedgerow and the little cock robin swelled out his red throat and sang a song for the little hen robin. She was so pleased that she said she would marry him and build a nest.

So they hunted up and down the hedgerow for a good place. At the bottom was a ditch full of dead leaves.

'These leaves would be splendid for making a nest,' sang the cock robin.

'So will this moss!' sang the hen, pulling some out with her beak in delight.

'Look! Here is a fine hole in the bank!' trilled the cock, excitedly. 'Shall we build here?'

The hen flew up and looked inside the hole. It had been an old wasps' nest the year before. A tiny mouse had been inside and gobbled up anything that still remained. Now the hole was empty. It faced the right way, and was well hidden under the overhanging hedge. The hen robin was pleased with it.

Together the robins built their nest. They wove a few tiny twigs together, they twisted in some grass roots and they brought green and brown moss to tuck in the cracks. The cock robin found nice dry leaves in the ditch and decorated the nest beautifully with them. When he had finished you could hardly see the nest at all, for it matched the ditch and the bank so well, with its moss and dead leaves!

'Now,' said the little hen robin happily, 'I shall lay some eggs. Then we'll have some tiny robin chicks to love. Won't it be fun!'

But before she could lay any eggs, a dreadful thing

happened! The farmer's son came along that way, looking for nests, because he wanted to collect eggs for himself. First he looked in the hedgerow and found a hedge sparrow's nest with three blue eggs in and he took all those. Then he looked down on the bank and saw the little hen robin sitting close on her new nest.

'Shoo! Shoo!' cried the boy unkindly. The robin flew off, frightened, and from a nearby bush the cock robin sang angrily at the horrid boy.

The boy bent down to see if there were any eggs in the robin's nest, and when he saw there were none, he flew into a rage. He kicked at the pretty nest and it flew to pieces! The bits of moss, the grass roots and the dead leaves fell to the ditch below – and that was the end of the little nest that had taken the robins a whole week to build.

The little birds were sorrowful. When the boy had gone they hopped around the place where their nest had been and grieved bitterly.

'It is such a good thing there were no eggs in it,' sang the little hen robin. 'Suppose he had taken them! How sad we would have been then!'

'I don't like that boy!' trilled the cock robin. 'Let us build our next nest in some place where he never goes.'

So they hunted around once more – and then, in a field on the farm they found an old kettle with its lid gone. The cock robin perched near the hole where the lid had once fitted and sang to his mate.

'Here is a good place! This hole will take a nest very nicely! We shall be safe here. Come, let us bring moss and leaves, and build again in this friendly old kettle.'

So once more the two little redbreasts began to build. How hard they worked! The days were warm, and the little hen robin was anxious to lay eggs and bring up her chicks. Soon the nest inside the kettle was finished. It was very cosy indeed. You could hardly see it unless you looked inside. Only some dry grass and a strand of moss peeped out of it, and when the hen robin sat inside just her beak could be seen.

She laid four pretty red-brown eggs. The two little birds were so pleased and proud. The hen robin sat on them all day long to keep them warm, and the cock robin roamed about to find dainty titbits to bring to her. He sang to her too, and she listened. When it rained she tucked herself down into the kettle and fluffed her feathers well out so that her precious eggs should not get wet.

Now, one day the farmer himself walked over the field. He had planted seeds there, and the birds had been busy eating some of them. The farmer was very angry indeed. He clapped his hands at the rooks there, and shooed the jackdaws. But the birds cawed and took no notice.

'I shall put up a scarecrow,' said the farmer, in a rage. 'That will keep all the birds away! Drat them! Not one of those birds is an atom of good to a farmer!'

Well, of course, that's where he was wrong. It was true that some of his seeds were eaten, but dear me, if only he could have seen how many harmful grubs, beetles and caterpillars the birds ate too, how surprised he would have been!

He walked along by the side of the field, grumbling. When he came up to the kettle, the sun shone out and made it shine here and there, though most of it was very rusty. The farmer looked at it and frowned.

'How many times am I to tell people not to throw their old kettles, saucepans and tins on my fields!' he shouted angrily. 'I won't have it!'

He picked up the kettle. It seemed heavy so he looked inside – and as he looked, the little hen robin, who had been sitting on her eggs, flew out in a fright. She almost flew into the farmer's face and she made him jump.

'Another bird!' shouted the farmer, and he shook his fist. 'It's got its nest in the kettle too – well it can go and nest somewhere else!'

With that he threw the old kettle over the hedge

into the garden of one of the cottages nearby and stamped off, saying, 'Yes, a scarecrow is what is needed, no doubt of that at all!'

The kettle crashed to the ground and the nest was spilt out in a heap.

The two robins were nearly broken-hearted. They sat close together in the hedge, and looked mournfully down at their eggs.

'First the farmer's son, and then the farmer!' said the cock robin. 'Are we never to have a nest and eggs in safety? Wherever shall we build now?'

'I don't feel as if I want to build any more,' sighed the little hen robin. But the cock robin nestled close to her and cheered her up. 'We'll find a good place!' he sang. 'Don't fear! We shall be lucky the third time!'

Now, the next day along came the farmer and put up a most fearsome-looking scarecrow in the middle of the field. It had a carved-out turnip for a head, an old hat, a raggedy coat and scarf and a pair of the farmer's oldest trousers. It had wooden sticks for arms and legs and really, when the farmer had finished putting it up, it looked for all the world like a scary old man standing guard right in the middle of the field!

All the birds there were frightened. They really thought it was a friend of the farmer's, and when the wind blew the coat to and fro, they flew away in terror. The robins were frightened too.

'Do you think that horrible man will come after us and find our nest and eggs when we build and lay once more?' asked the hen robin fearfully.

'I will go and ask him if he means to harm us,' said the cock robin bravely. 'If he says yes, we will fly away to another place and build there.'

So off he flew to the scarecrow in the very middle of the field. He perched on its hat and spoke to it.

'Do you mean to spoil our nests?' he asked.

The scarecrow looked at the little robin out of his big turnip eyes. The tiny bird saw that he had a kind face, though very strange.

'Why should I want to spoil your nest?' said the scarecrow in astonishment. 'I wish no one harm. I would like to be friendly with all birds and beasts for I am very lonely out here all by myself, shunned by everyone. But no one ever comes to say how-do-you-do, or to wish me goodnight.'

The robin looked at the scarecrow's gentle face in surprise. 'You are not really the farmer's friend then?' he asked.

'Oh, no,' said the scarecrow. 'He is a rough, bad-tempered man. I am sorry to have to work for him – but what can I do? I cannot get up and walk away, you know. Here I must stay, day and night, cold, lonely and miserable.'

The cock robin called his little wife and told her that the scarecrow was a gentle, friendly creature, who would certainly not harm them or their eggs.

The hen robin sang her best song to the scarecrow and he was delighted. 'Do build your nest somewhere really safe this time,' he begged. 'I should be so unhappy if I knew that once more your nest had been spoilt.'

'I can't think where to build this time,' said the cock robin. 'I've hunted everywhere, and nowhere seems really safe.'

For a few minutes the scarecrow said nothing at all – but suddenly his big turnip face lit up and he shook with excitement.

'Friends!' he said. 'I know the safest place in the world for you! The very, very safest!'

'Where is that?' asked the robins.

'In the pocket of my coat!' said the old scarecrow, his kind face still beaming. 'No one would ever think of looking there, not even the farmer himself! Not a person in the world would guess that any bird was daring enough to nest in the pocket of a scarecrow! Oh, do build your nest there, little friends. You can't think how happy it would make me. I should no longer be lonely or unhappy.'

The robins flew down to the coat and peeped at the

pocket. It was a big one, and gaped open. It was really just exactly right for a nest! The robins stared at one another excitedly.

'The scarecrow's right!' sang the little cock robin. 'He's right! This is a good place, a safe one, where we can be unseen. Let us nest here!'

So they began to build their nest in the pocket of the scarecrow's raggedy coat. They filled it with soft moss, roots and leaves, and then the little hen robin cuddled inside and laid four more red-brown eggs.

How delighted the old scarecrow was! When the eggs hatched and the little chicks cheeped hungrily, he almost twisted his turnip head off, trying to look down to see what they were like! The old robins talked to him every day and sang their best song, for they were most grateful to him for his help.

One day the farmer's boy came along the field-path, and as he went he looked along the hedge and the bank.

'Where did those robins build?' he said in a

temper. 'They must have built somewhere again, and I have never found their eggs, after all. I suppose that scarecrow has frightened them away. What a pity! I could have found their eggs and taken them.'

'Did you hear that?' whispered the scarecrow to the two robins, who were closely cuddled inside his pocket, sitting over their young ones to keep them warm.

'Yes, we did!' trilled the robins. 'You were quite right, scarecrow – this was the very safest place of all! If you are here next year we'll come and build in your pocket again!'

Won't the scarecrow be pleased if they do! He was sad when the two old birds and the four young ones said goodbye – but they often go to see him, so he isn't nearly so lonely as he used to be, poor, gentle old scarecrow!

Whiskers and Balloon-Face

Whiskers and Balloon-Face

JENNIFER HUNG the big red balloon in her bedroom. It had a long string and hung down, swaying to and fro because it was so light. Jennifer had been to a party and every child had had a balloon.

The toys stared at the big balloon. They had never seen one before. The balloon had a face painted on it, and the face smiled and smiled. The toys rather liked it.

But they were afraid of the balloon and not one of them went near it, not even the toy lion, who was the boldest of the lot.

Jennifer went off to school. The toys were left alone

in the bedroom. The balloon swung gently to and fro, because the window was open and a little breeze came blowing in.

Someone jumped in at the window. The toys looked at the someone in dismay. It was Whiskers, the next-door cat. The toys didn't like Whiskers. He sometimes came in and stole the milk out of the milk jug. He chased the clockwork mouse all round the room. And once he had rolled a skittle over and over so long that the skittle had felt ill for a week.

'There's Whiskers!' whispered the lion to the teddy bear. 'Where's the clockwork mouse? Quick! Tell him to hide inside the brick box.'

'I hope he doesn't scratch off my new hat,' said the doll. 'He's a horrid cat. I wish he didn't keep coming here.'

'Hallo, toys!' said Whiskers, looking around. 'You don't seem very pleased to see me! Say hallo!'

'Hallo, Whiskers,' said all the toys obediently.

Then Whiskers caught sight of the big balloon swaying in the breeze. He saw the smiling face on the balloon and he thought it was another toy.

'I didn't hear you say hallo!' Whiskers said rather fiercely to the balloon.

The balloon swayed a little and grinned hard. It didn't say a word, of course.

'Now look here!' said Whiskers, seeing that all the toys were laughing at him. 'Now look here – you've got to be polite to me! I'm Whiskers, the king of all the cats around here!'

He turned back to the balloon. 'What's your name?' he said.

The balloon didn't answer. Whiskers spat at it angrily and the balloon swayed a little more. The face went on smiling and Whiskers felt angry. 'Take that smile off your face!' he said. 'If you don't, I will! Stop grinning at me like that!'

The balloon went on smiling. Whiskers suddenly hit out with a paw, and the balloon swung right back and then bobbed forward and bumped Whiskers on the nose.

Whiskers felt a little alarmed. He backed away a bit and the lion laughed loudly. Whiskers ran at him and he dived into the toy cupboard and hid under the big kite there.

Whiskers walked away from the cupboard looking so fierce that all the toys trembled. The clockwork mouse felt safe in the brick box though, and shouted after him, in his squeaky voice, 'Yah, yah! You're afraid of the balloon-face! It's laughing at you! It thinks you are a silly cat!'

Whiskers hissed in rage and looked all about for the clockwork mouse. But he had bobbed down safely in the brick box and could not be seen. Whiskers walked to the balloon again.

'You may think it's funny to bob about and grin like that,' he said, 'but it isn't! It's silly. You be polite and tell me your name.'

The balloon didn't say a word, which wasn't

surprising because it never had and never would. The wind blew in at the window and swung it against Whiskers' ears.

'Don't do that,' said Whiskers fiercely. 'Are you trying to bite my ears? Keep away or I'll scratch you!'

'Ho, ho!' laughed the toys. 'The balloon isn't afraid of you, Whiskers! You're afraid of old balloon-face!'

'I am not!' said Whiskers. 'I am afraid of nothing, not even of the great big dog across the road. He runs away when he sees me.'

'Oh, fibber!' cried the doll. The balloon swung up into the air in the wind and came down on Whiskers' tail.

'How dare you try to pull my tail?' said Whiskers, swinging his long tail angrily from side to side. 'Stop grinning like that, I tell you. It's rude!'

The balloon-face went on smiling broadly. Whiskers lost his temper and lashed out with his right paw, all his sharp claws sticking out.

One of the claws went into the big balloon. Bang!

The balloon wasn't there any more! Only a bit of red rubber hung down from the string.

Whiskers leapt high into the air.

The toys all dived into the toy cupboard and shut the door when they heard the loud bang. They sat and shivered inside, wondering what had happened to the smiling balloon It just said 'Bang!' and disappeared. It was most extraordinary.

Jennifer came back from school at that moment and heard the bang. She ran into her bedroom, and saw Whiskers and the burst balloon.

'You bad, wicked cat!' she shouted at him, almost in tears. 'You've burst my balloon.'

Whiskers jumped out of the window in fright, and the toys heard him wailing outside in the garden.

'He won't come back again!' said the lion, poking his head out of the cupboard.

He didn't. Jennifer took down the balloon string and bit of rubber and threw them sadly away. She knew what had happened but the toys didn't.

'Where did balloon-face go to?' they kept asking one another. 'He said "Bang!" and went. Where did he go to?'

Perhaps Jennifer will tell them, or maybe she will bring home another balloon. I hope it won't go pop, don't you?

The New Little Calves

The New Little Calves

ONE DAY Jenny came running to Billy in great excitement. 'Billy! What do you think's happened? Buttercup the cow has got twin calves!'

'Twins!' said Billy in surprise. 'Oh, where are they?'

The children went to see the new calves. They were exactly alike. Billy stared at them in delight.

'No horns,' he said. 'And what long, long legs. Aren't they sweet?'

'Look,' said Jenny, and she put her hand to one calf's mouth. It began to suck it at once. Billy let the other calf suck his. It was a tickly feeling. The calf looked at him out of soft brown eyes.

'You dear little thing,' said Billy. 'I wish you were mine. Oh, Jenny, do you think Aunt Susan would let me look after this calf? I do love it.'

'Buttercup, its mother, will look after it at first,' said Jenny. 'But if you like you can help to teach it to drink milk later on. I'll show you how.'

The two calves grew very fast. In no time at all they were walking about on long, rather wobbly legs, and they always went to meet the children when they saw them coming.

Then the day came when they were to be taught how to drink milk from a pail. 'Come along, Billy, and I'll show you,' said Jenny.

Billy went with her, and the two calves followed. Jenny got two pails of skim-milk from her mother, and then smiled at Billy.

'Now, you do what I do,' she said, 'and we'll soon teach these calves.'

'But why do they have to be taught?' asked Billy. 'Why don't we just let them drink the milk?'

'Because they don't know how to,' said Jenny. 'They can only suck. Drinking is different.'

Billy watched her. She put her pail down and knelt beside it. One little calf nuzzled up to her. Jenny dipped her fingers into the milk and held them out to the calf.

It sniffed the milk on them and licked them. Then it sucked them. Jenny dipped her fingers into the milk again and the same thing happened. Then again and again the little girl dipped in her hand and the calf licked and sucked.

'Now watch, Billy,' said Jenny. 'I'm gradually going to hold my hand nearer and nearer to the milk in the pail – and soon, when the calf bends its head down to lick my fingers, it will find that my hand is touching the milk in the pail – and then I'll have my hand so close to the milk that it will be licking my fingers *and* licking the milk in the pail at the same time!'

Billy watched – and, sure enough, Jenny held her hand nearer and nearer to the milk – until at last the calf had to put its head right down into the pail to find Jenny's hand – and, dear me, where *was* her hand? It was in the milk! So in the end the calf found that it was licking up the milk in the pail – it was drinking!

'There you are,' said Jenny, smiling. 'I've taught him to drink already! I'll have to teach him again tomorrow and the next day, because he'll forget – but in no time at all he'll come running out when he sees me with the pail of milk, and he'll put in his head and drink the lot!'

Jenny was right, of course. It wasn't long before her little trick had taught the hungry calves to drink properly.

And now you should see them each morning when Billy and Jenny come out with their pails. Up come the two little calves at once, and how they drink and drink and drink!

The Careless Hedgehogs

The Careless Hedgehogs

ONCE UPON a time, Hoo, the white owl, found a baby elf cuddled up in his nest.

'Tu-whit!' he said, most astonished. 'Who are you?'

The baby elf stared at him, but didn't answer a word.

Hoo perched on the side of his nest, and wondered what he should do with the strange little creature.

'I'll go and ask my friend Prickles,' he said at last. 'He is wise, and will tell me.'

Off he flew.

Prickles, the hedgehog, was awake, just outside his house.

'Good evening,' said Hoo politely.

'Good evening,' answered Prickles. 'Why have you come to see me?'

'In my nest there is a strange little elf that will not speak a word,' explained Hoo. 'What am I to do with it?'

'A little elf!' said Prickles, sitting up quickly. 'What is it like?'

'It is small, with yellow wings,' answered Hoo.

'Have you seen the notice the king of Fairyland has put up everywhere?' asked Prickles excitedly.

'No,' said Hoo.

'Come and I'll show it to you,' said Prickles, scuttling off.

Presently they came to a tall foxglove. Hanging upon it was a notice which said,

LOST FROM DREAMLAND:

A LITTLE ELF BABY WITH YELLOW

WINGS. ANYONE FINDING IT SHALL

THE CARELESS HEDGEHOGS

HAVE A GREAT REWARD.

PLEASE TELL THE

KING OF FAIRYLAND

'There!' said Prickles. 'You must have found the lost baby elf.'

'But how could it have got into my nest?' asked Hoo, very puzzled.

'Don't bother about *that*!' answered Prickles. 'Go and tell the king you've found it!'

'Will you take care of it while I'm gone?' asked Hoo.

'Yes,' said Prickles. 'I'll get all the fairy hedgehogs I know to look after it.'

So Hoo flew down to the hedgehogs, carrying the elf baby gently.

'Now look after it carefully,' he said, flying off to the king's palace.

All the fairy hedgehogs sat down in a ring, and looked at the baby. It lay in the middle of them and laughed and kicked.

'I think perhaps the bad gnomes stole it,' said Prickles. 'They are enemies to the people of Dreamland.'

Whenever anyone came near the little baby, the hedgehogs stiffened all their prickles, and made the very worst noise they could.

'Here comes Hoo!' cried Prickles at last. Hoo perched on the tree above him.

'It *is* the lost baby,' he cried, 'and the king of Dreamland is coming to fetch it in two days. Our king says you must take great care of it till then, and give it honey to eat and dew to drink.'

'Very well,' said Prickles.

'And,' said Hoo, flying off, 'you must see that the bad gnomes don't come for it again.'

So all that day the hedgehogs watched the elf baby. Prickles fetched it honey from the heather and dew from the grasses. All through the night the fairy hedgehogs watched, and next day Prickles said, 'I'm going to fetch a special dew from the red blackberry leaves. Be very careful while I am gone.'

Off he went.

Then one of the little hedgehogs stretched itself.

'I'm *so* tired of watching,' he said, 'I'm going off for a little walk.'

He ran off through the grass, but in a minute he came back looking very excited.

'Come quickly!' he cried. 'There is a fairy dance by the foxgloves tonight, and if we're quick we can all go and hear the music.'

The hedgehogs thought that would be lovely.

'We'll go to the dance till Prickles comes back!' they cried. 'He'll never know.'

Off they scampered as hard as they could, and were soon having a glorious time.

The little elf baby, finding there was nobody to stop it, crawled away by itself, and fell fast asleep under a mushroom a little way off.

Suddenly there was a great fluttering of wings, and down flew the king of Dreamland and the king of Fairyland; they had come to fetch the lost elf baby.

At the same moment up came Prickles too, with his blackberry dew for the baby.

'Where is the baby?' cried the king of Dreamland.

'I don't know,' answered Prickles, looking astonished. 'It was here when I left, guarded by lots of fairy hedgehogs. Now they're all gone!'

At that moment, back came the hedgehogs from the dance. They looked very frightened when they saw that the baby was gone and the two kings had come.

'How *dare* you disobey my orders?' said the king of Fairyland to the trembling hedgehogs. 'Now the baby has gone again, and perhaps the bad gnomes have stolen it away just because you weren't watching!'

'Please, we're very sorry,' said the hedgehogs.

'That doesn't help matters,' said the Dreamland king angrily.

'I shall have to punish you,' said the fairy king. 'You haven't been good hedgehogs, so perhaps you will be good if I change you into something else!'

He waved his hand. In a minute all the fairy

hedgehogs found themselves climbing up a big chestnut tree.

The king waved his wand again.

The hedgehogs climbed along the branches, turned green, and sat quite still.

'There!' said the king. 'Now perhaps they will keep the baby chestnuts from harm until they're ripe. Now, Prickles, hunt around until you find the elf baby.'

Of course Prickles found him under the mushroom very quickly, and brought him back to the king of Dreamland.

But Prickles is very lonely now without the other hedgehogs. They never come down to play with him, because they are so busy looking after the baby chestnuts, and they are much more careful of them than they were of the little elf baby.

And if you look at a chestnut tree in October, you'll see what the king changed the hedgehogs into – and you'll find they're still very prickly!

Micky's Present

Micky's Present

ONE DAY Miss Brown, the children's schoolteacher, spoke to the children rather sadly.

'You will be sorry to hear that poor little Ronnie is very ill,' she said. 'He will have to stay in bed at least two months.'

The children were sorry. 'Can we do anything to make things nicer for him?' asked Jane, who was always the first to be kind.

'Well,' said Miss Brown, 'you might buy him a book or two when you have the money – or jigsaw puzzles perhaps. Something like that. It will be very dull for the poor little boy.'

Micky listened to what Miss Brown said. He was very fond of Ronnie, because he and Ronnie loved the same things. They never wanted to go into the hot, stuffy cinema on Saturdays as so many of the others did – they loved to go out together into the country lanes and fields and watch the birds and animals there.

Once they had seen a grey squirrel hiding his nuts. Another time they had found a prickly hedgehog, and he had rolled himself up into a ball as soon as he had seen them coming. They often listened to the birds singing, and Micky told Ronnie what they all were. They watched the rabbits playing in the evening, and had a much better time than the children who had gone to the cinema.

Micky felt very sorry for Ronnie. Now he wouldn't be able to watch the birds and animals as he loved to do. *I shall miss him dreadfully*, thought Micky. *I will take him a present.*

But Micky had no money to buy a present. He

didn't even get ten pence a week, because his mother was very poor. Micky asked her if he could have some money to get Ronnie a book or a puzzle.

'I haven't the money to spare,' said his mother. 'You know I had to buy you a pair of new boots last week, Micky.'

'Well, Mother, couldn't you even spare me some money for a *Sunny Stories*?' asked Micky. 'I could just get that for Ronnie. He does so like the stories in it, you know.'

'Not twenty, not ten, not even one penny,' said his mother firmly. 'If you want to give Ronnie something, you must give him one of your own toys.'

Micky went to look at his toys – but, dear me, they were a very poor, broken lot! *They're not fit to give to anybody*, thought poor Micky. He sat and wondered about Ronnie. It must be horrid to lie in bed day after day, with only the clouds to watch moving in the sky. How he would miss the birds he loved!

And then, as Micky sat and thought, such a

splendid idea came to him. He leapt up and clapped his hands.

'Of course! I'll make him a bird table and fix it up just outside his bedroom window if his mother will let me! I'll put food on it every day for the birds, and Ronnie can lie and watch them and be happy.'

Making a bird table didn't cost Micky even one penny. He took a piece of wood from the shed, and looked about for a stick for a leg. His mother gave him an old broom handle. Just the thing! He nailed the flat piece of wood on to the leg. There was the table!

He put it over his shoulder and marched off to Ronnie's house. Ronnie's bedroom was downstairs. Micky saw Mrs Leslie in the garden, and he spoke to her.

'Please, Mrs Leslie,' he said, 'I've got a present for your Ronnie. It's a bird table. May I put it up just outside his window? He does so love the birds, you know.'

'How very kind of you, Micky!' said Mrs Leslie. 'Poor old Ronnie feels so dull now, lying in bed day after day. He is tired of his books and puzzles. He will love to watch the birds.'

Micky put up the table just outside Ronnie's window. Ronnie was fast asleep, so Micky tried not to make any noise. He dug a hole for the broom handle, and then fixed it hard in the earth, treading it down firmly. The top of the table was just above Ronnie's windowsill. He would be able to see the birds beautifully when they came.

'Mrs Leslie, I'll go out into the lanes each Saturday and find some things that the birds love to eat,' said Micky. 'They'll love berries, you know, and seeds of all kinds. I'll collect lots! And I'll ask my uncle for one of his big sunflower heads – that can go on the table too. The birds will come to peck out the seeds. And if I can get a few monkey nuts, I will. The tits love those.'

'You're a kind fellow, Micky,' said Mrs Leslie. 'Ronnie will be so pleased.'

Micky ran home, wondering what Ronnie would say when he woke up. And what *did* Ronnie say? He was simply delighted! His mother had spread some crumbs on the table, and already one robin and three sparrows were hopping there.

'Mother! Who gave me that?' cried Ronnie in delight. 'Oh, what fine fun I shall have every day watching my birds! I shall soon know every one.'

Each day the table was spread with bits and pieces – bones for the starlings, bread for the robins, scraps for the sparrows, bits of potato for the thrushes and blackbirds. They all came and pecked hungrily. Then Micky brought berries and seeds – and you should have seen how the birds loved those!

When the doctor came in two weeks' time he was surprised to see how much better Ronnie was looking.

'He seems so bright and happy,' he said to Mrs Leslie. 'That is splendid.'

'Look – this is what keeps him so interested and happy,' said Mrs Leslie, and she showed the doctor the bird table. On it were seven starlings, four sparrows, one robin, two chaffinches, three tits, one blackbird and one thrush – and really, the table could hardly hold any more!

'What a good idea!' said the doctor. 'No wonder Ronnie looks so bright. I really think, Mrs Leslie, that he might have a friend to tea next week, just to cheer him up a bit.'

Ronnie was so pleased – and whom do you suppose he asked to come to tea? Yes, Mickey, of course, and together the two friends watched the birds having their tea at the same time.

'It was kind of you to give me such a lovely present as that, Micky,' said Ronnie.

'Well, it wasn't much of a present,' said Micky. 'It didn't cost even a penny.'

'It's the nicest present of the lot!' said Ronnie. 'You took the trouble to think of what I really would love, Micky – and I do love it too. It's my favourite present.'

It was rather a good present, wasn't it? It would be

lovely if every girl and boy could have a bird table to watch – they really are such fun!

Bushy's Secret

Bushy's Secret

THIS IS the story of a secret.

It was Bushy Squirrel's secret, and the secret was where he had hidden his nuts.

He had hidden them in the hollow oak tree, and covered them with leaves. He thought it was such a clever place to think of.

'Nobody will ever look there,' he said. 'It's a secret, a secret, a secret! It's fun to have a secret! I won't tell anyone!'

'What won't you tell anyone?' asked Chitter-Chatter the magpie, who came flying by and heard Bushy talking to himself.

'I shan't tell anyone my secret!' said Bushy.

'Oh, do tell me,' said Chitter-Chatter. 'I won't tell anyone!' So Bushy told him. He whispered his secret in Chitter-Chatter's little ear.

'This is my secret,' he said. 'I've hidden my nuts in the hollow oak tree. Isn't it a clever place?'

'Very,' said Chitter-Chatter, and flew off again.

Presently Chitter-Chatter spied Bobtail Bunny frisking down below, and he flew down to him.

'Good morning, Bobtail,' he said. 'I've just seen Bushy Squirrel. He's got a secret, and he told it to me.'

'A secret! Oh, do tell me!' begged Bobtail. 'I won't tell anyone!'

So Chitter-Chatter whispered the secret in Bobtail's soft ear.

'This is Bushy's secret,' he said. 'He's hidden his nuts in the hollow oak tree. Isn't it a clever place?'

'Very!' said Bobtail, and scampered off.

He soon saw Prickles the hedgehog running along by a hedge, and he scampered up to him.

'Good morning, Prickles!' he said. 'I've just seen Chitter-Chatter the magpie. He knows a secret, and he told it to me!'

'A secret! Oh, do tell me!' begged Prickles. 'I won't tell anyone!'

So Bobtail Bunny whispered the secret in Prickles's spiky ear.

'This is the secret,' he said. 'Someone, I won't tell who, has hidden his nuts in the hollow oak tree. Isn't it a clever place?'

'Very!' said Prickles, and ran off.

He soon met Frisky Squirrel, Bushy's cousin, and he hurried up to him.

'Good morning, Frisky,' he said. 'I've just seen Bobtail Bunny. He knows a secret and he told it to me.'

'A secret! Oh, do tell me!' begged Frisky. 'I won't tell anyone!'

So Prickles the hedgehog whispered the secret in Frisky's ear.

'This is the secret,' he said. 'Someone has hidden his

nuts in the hollow oak tree. Isn't it a clever place?'

'Very!' said Frisky, and leapt away to the hollow oak tree.

On his way he met Bushy Squirrel.

'Good morning, Bushy,' he said. 'I've just seen Prickles the hedgehog. He knows a secret, and he told it to me.'

'A secret! How lovely! I've got a secret too!' said Bushy. 'Do tell me the secret you know! I won't tell anyone!'

So Frisky whispered the secret in Bushy's sharp ear.

'This is the secret,' he said. 'Someone has hidden his nuts in the hollow oak tree! Isn't it a clever place? Come along and find them, Bushy! We'll have a lovely feast!'

'But that's my secret!' wailed Bushy. 'It's my secret! They're my nuts! I thought no one would think of such a clever place!'

'Oh, everybody knows!' said Frisky in surprise. 'Prickles told me. I forget who told Prickles.'

'I'm going to ask him,' said Bushy crossly and off he went.

'Who told you my secret, Prickles?' he asked when he found him.

'Bobtail Bunny did,' said Prickles, 'but I forget who told him.'

Bushy went to find Bobtail Bunny.

'Who told you my secret, Bobtail?' he asked when he found him.

'Chitter-Chatter the magpie did!' said Bobtail. 'He said you told him your secret, Bushy!'

'So I did, so I did!' said Bushy. 'And I wish I hadn't. Oh, dear, dear me! I suppose I must go and hide my nuts somewhere else now!'

But when he looked for them, they were gone! That rascally squirrel Frisky had taken them.

'And all because nobody could keep a secret!' wept poor Bushy. 'Well, I'll remember next time that the only way to keep a secret is to keep it yourself!'

The Tale of Flop and Whiskers

The Tale of Flop and Whiskers

FLOP AND Whiskers were two white rabbits belonging to Malcolm and Jean. They had fine whiskers, little black bobtails and big floppy ears. Malcolm and Jean were very fond of them and looked after them well.

Flop and Whiskers lived happily enough in a big cage. They were friendly with one another, but sometimes they found things dull.

'Oh, if only something exciting would happen!' Flop would sigh.

'Yes, something that we could remember and talk about for weeks and weeks,' said Whiskers.

'But nothing ever happens to pet rabbits. We just live in a cage and eat and sleep. That's all.'

But one night something *did* happen! Flop and Whiskers heard a noise in the garden, and looked out of their cage. It was bright moonlight and coming down the garden path was a long procession of fairies. In their midst was a snow-white carriage with gold handles and gold wheels. It was drawn by six rabbits.

'Just look at that!' cried Flop excitedly. 'It must be a fairy princess of some kind. Oh, don't I wish I was one of those rabbits pulling her carriage! Wouldn't I feel grand!'

'Isn't it beautiful?' said Whiskers, his little nose pressed against the wires of the cage.

The procession came down the path and passed by the rabbits' cage. They were so excited. They could see a golden-haired princess in the carriage and just as she passed their cage she leant out and blew a kiss to them. Flop scraped at the wire of the cage, trying her hardest to get out and run after the procession –

but it was no use, the wire was too strong.

'Look!' suddenly cried Whiskers. 'The procession has stopped. What has happened?'

'Oh, dear! One of the rabbits has gone lame,' said Flop. 'See, its foot is limping.'

What a to-do there was! All the fairies gathered round the limping rabbit, who shook his head dolefully and held up his foot in pain.

The princess leant out of her carriage and pointed to the rabbit-hutch she had just passed. She called out something in her high little voice.

'I say, Flop, I believe the princess is saying that one of us could draw her carriage instead of the rabbit with the poorly foot!' said Whiskers in excitement. 'Oh, I wonder which of us will be chosen.'

The little fairies came running back to the cage and climbed up to the wire.

'Will you come and draw our princess's carriage just for tonight?' they cried. 'One of our rabbits has hurt its foot.'

'Oh yes!' squeaked the two white rabbits in delight. 'But which of us do you want?'

'Both of you, please,' said the fairies. 'You see, the rabbits have to go in pairs. We shall set free the hurt rabbit and his companion. So will you both come? You shall be brought back before sunrise.'

Flop and Whiskers joyfully told the fairies how to open their cage and then they jumped out in delight. In a trice they were harnessed with the other rabbits, and the two whose place they were taking hopped away into the hedges. The fairies cried out in delight to see the two beautiful new rabbits.

They made such a noise that they woke up Malcolm and Jean. The children jumped out of bed and went to their bedroom window, looking out into the moonlight.

They saw the fairy procession going along down the garden path and they stared in astonishment.

'Jean!' said Malcolm. 'Look at those two white rabbits with black tails, drawing the carriage. Don't they look like Flop and Whiskers?'

'Yes, they do,' said Jean. 'And oh, look! Malcolm, their cage door is open. I can see it quite plainly in the moonlight.'

The children ran downstairs to see the procession, but it had passed by before they were in the garden. So they went to see if the rabbit cage was open – and it was.

'Oh, dear, I *shall* be sorry not to have dear old Flop and Whiskers,' said Jean, almost crying. 'They were so sweet. I don't think it was very kind of the fairies to take them away from us.'

But the next morning the cage door was fast shut and the two white rabbits were safely back in their hutch once more! When Malcolm and Jean went to peep, they found both rabbits fast asleep in the hay, and they didn't even wake when the children put some fresh lettuce in for them.

'Goodness, aren't they tired!' said Jean. 'I expect they walked for miles last night, dragging that lovely carriage behind them. I do wonder where they went.'

Flop and Whiskers longed to tell the children all about their adventures, but they couldn't. When they woke up they looked at one another in delight, and Flop said, 'Did we dream it, Whiskers, or was it true?'

'Quite true,' said Whiskers. 'We've had an adventure at last, Flop. We can talk about it for weeks and weeks, and we'll never feel dull again.'

So they talk about it all day long – and I wish I could listen to them, don't you?

Where Was Baby Pam?

Where Was Baby Pam?

BABY PAM was nearly two years old, and she could walk all over the place. Billie, her brother, and Susie, her sister, were very proud of her. So was her mother. She was such a happy baby, and everyone loved her.

Now, one day, when the sun was shining brightly into the kitchen, Mother began to bake some cakes. Baby Pam watched her. She watched the sunshine too, coming in at the doorway.

She walked to the door and looked out. Her mother was busy and didn't miss her. She put one little foot out of doors and then the other – and in a moment she had gone from the kitchen to look for the sunshine.

In a few minutes Mother looked round to see where Baby Pam was. She wasn't there! Mother looked under the table. She wasn't there either, hiding from her mother.

'Oh, dear,' said Mother, 'where has she gone?'

She ran to the door and looked out. She couldn't see the baby anywhere. Billie and Susie were playing among the bushes at the end of the garden, Rover was lying in his kennel, half asleep, and Puss-Cat was on the wall, washing herself. Wherever was Baby Pam?

'Billie! Susie!' called Mother. 'Is Pam with you?'

Billie and Susie came running up the garden.

'No!' they cried. 'We haven't seen her. Wasn't she in the kitchen with you, Mummy?'

'Yes,' said Mother, looking worried, 'she was. But I suddenly missed her and now I can't find her anywhere. It's time for her morning sleep too. Wherever can she have got to? Look all over the garden, there's good children!'

Billie and Susie ran all over the garden calling Baby

Pam. 'Pam! Pam! Baby Pam!' they called. But no little girl came running to meet them. It was very odd.

'Has she gone out into the street, do you think?' asked Billie. 'The back gate is quite easy to open.'

'Oh, go and look,' said his mother. 'I do hope she hasn't.'

Billie ran to see – but there was nobody in the road at all. Pam wasn't there.

'No, she's not there, Mummy,' said Billie, coming back. 'She must be in the garden then. But where? We've looked simply everywhere!'

'Have you looked in the garden shed?' asked Susie. 'Come on – let's look there. I remember hiding there once when I was little.'

They ran to the garden shed and opened the door. It was quite dark inside. They called 'Pam! Pam!' loudly – but no one was there. They shut the door and looked at one another in dismay.

'Isn't it funny!' said Billie. 'She must be somewhere. She can't just vanish.'

'You don't suppose the goblins have taken her, do you?' asked Susie.

'Of course not! Don't be silly. The goblins never come here. I know! Perhaps she has gone out of the back gate and into Mrs Brown's next door. Let's go and ask.'

They ran down the path and out into the road. They went through the next gate and knocked at the front door. Mrs Brown opened the door, and was very much surprised to see Billie and Susie looking so hot and bothered.

'Is Pam here?' asked Susie.

'No, my dear,' answered Mrs Brown. 'Dear, dear, I hope you haven't lost her.'

'Yes, we have!' said Susie, beginning to cry. 'Whatever shall we do? We've looked simply everywhere.'

'Why don't you go and get Rover, your dog, to help you?' said Mrs Brown. 'He could soon follow her footsteps and find her for you.'

'Oh yes, what a good idea!' cried Billie. 'Come on, Susie, let's go and call him.'

They ran back home. As soon as they were in their own garden they called Rover.

'Hi, Rover, Rover! Come here!' they called.

Rover opened one eye and looked at them.

'Come on, quickly, Rover!' shouted Billie. 'You're not tied up. Come on!'

Rover raised his head and yawned. Billie felt cross.

'Rover!' he cried. 'Will you do as you're told! Come here at once. We want you to look for Baby Pam.'

Rover pricked up his ears when he heard Billie say 'Baby Pam', but still he didn't move. He didn't even get up. He just sat there, half in and half out of his kennel, blinking at Billie and Susie.

The children ran up to him and caught hold of his collar. 'Don't you understand, Rover?' they cried. 'We want you to help us to find Baby Pam. She's lost.'

They tugged at his collar to make him get out of his kennel – but he wouldn't budge. Instead, to their enormous surprise, he growled at them!

'Rover! You growled at us!' said Susie, astonished.

'You've never done that before. Oh, you unkind dog! Get out of your kennel quickly. Mummy! Mummy! Come and get Rover out. He's growling at us.'

Mother came running out, looking more worried than ever. She had hunted upstairs and downstairs but still there was no sign of little Pam. She took hold of Rover's collar and pulled him out of the kennel – and then she gave a cry of surprise.

'Look!' she said, pointing inside the kennel. 'Do look!'

The children looked – and there, fast asleep on Rover's blanket, was Baby Pam, hidden in the kennel! She was very fond of the old dog and had gone there to play with him – and then had fallen asleep in his kennel!

'No wonder Rover wouldn't come out when you tried to make him!' said Mother. 'He was guarding Pam. He knew she was safe in his kennel, and he couldn't understand what all the fuss was about. Good old Rover!'

Mother patted him and he wagged his tail hard. Then Mother gently lifted Baby Pam off the blanket and took her, still sleeping, to her cot.

'What a good thing she's found!' said Susie, very glad. 'Let's go and tell Mrs Brown where she was after all. Won't she be surprised!'

And Mrs Brown certainly was!

The Runaway Mouse

The Runaway Mouse

DONALD HAD a pet mouse, which lived in a tiny cage on the nursery shelf. It was a white mouse with pink eyes, and was very pretty and tame. Donald was fond of it, and every day he carefully cleaned out its cage and gave it fresh food. He called the mouse Mickey, and the tiny thing would cuddle down in his hand and nuzzle its small nose between his fingers.

Now, one night, somehow or other, Mickey's cage door came open. Mickey walked to it and stuck his woffly nose out.

'Oho!' he said to himself. 'This is exciting. I can go out by myself in the wide world, and have adventures.'

He ran out of the door, scrambled down the shelf and found himself on the nursery floor. The toys were just waking up for their nightly play, and they *were* astonished to see Mickey the white mouse.

'Mickey,' they cried, 'what are you doing out of your cage? You will come to harm.'

'Not I,' said the mouse proudly. 'I am going to have adventures!'

'Well, you'll have them all right if you go near the cat!' growled the teddy bear. 'You silly creature! The only adventures *you'll* have are nasty ones. Be sensible and go back to your cage.'

'I won't!' said Mickey, woffling his nose hard. 'I tell you I am going to seek adventures. I want to be a hero mouse.'

'But think how sad poor Donald will be to find you gone in the morning,' said the toy clown.

'I'll be back by then!' said the silly little mouse. 'And what is this cat you are talking about? I'll go and find him and tell him *I'm* not afraid of him!'

'Well, you *are* silly, sillier even than I thought you were,' said the teddy bear. 'The cat will look at you, put out its paw, and then gobble you up.'

'Nonsense!' said the mouse. 'Well, I'm just going to have a word with the clockwork mouse before I start. Perhaps he would like to come with me.'

He ran over to the toy cupboard and went to where the clockwork mouse was just waking up. As soon as he had disappeared inside the cupboard, the toys began to talk to one another in low voices, so that Mickey could not hear them.

'What can we do to stop Mickey being so silly?' said the teddy.

'He'll be eaten, sure as eggs are eggs!' said the clown, putting his hands deep into his pockets.

'Donald will be very unhappy if he finds his mouse is gone,' said the golden-haired doll, and the dark-haired doll nodded her head.

'Well, we must stop him *some*how,' said the teddy bear. 'Let's think how!'

They all thought hard – and at last the clown took his hands out of his pockets and clapped them. 'I've thought,' he said. 'I've thought!'

'Tell us,' said all the others in excitement. The clown pulled them closer and whispered his plan.

'You know Donald's moneybox, don't you?' he began. 'Well, if we could get Mickey in there, we could shut down the lid and he'd be safe till the morning. It's Saturday tomorrow and Donald is sure to put a penny into the box. Mickey can squeak when he hears him putting the penny in, and when Donald opens the box he will find the mouse.'

'But there won't be air for him to breathe,' said the teddy bear.

'Oh yes, there will!' said the clown. 'What about the slit where you put the penny in? Plenty of air gets in through there.'

'But I don't see how we can get Mickey into the box,' said the golden-haired doll.

'Leave that to me!' said the clown. He saw the little

mouse coming out of the toy cupboard at that moment and he beckoned to him.

'Before you start out on your adventures, will you do something for us?' he asked. 'That is, if you are clever enough.'

'Of course I'm clever enough!' said the mouse sharply. 'What is it you want?'

'Well, we want to know how much money Donald has in his moneybox,' said the clown. 'We can't count money properly, and we wondered if a mouse could.'

'Oh, I expect I can,' said the mouse. 'Where's the moneybox?'

'Up on the shelf by your cage,' said the clown. 'I know where the key is. Come on.'

Everybody climbed up to the shelf, and the clown got the key, which was hidden in a little blue jar nearby. He unlocked the tin moneybox and lifted up the lid. Inside lay many pennies, a shilling and two sixpences. The mouse jumped inside the box and began to count.

'One penny, two pennies, three pennies–' and then

he stopped! The lid had shut with a bang, and there he was, trapped in the moneybox! He tried his hardest to lift up the lid, but oh, dear me, what was this he heard? It was the clown carefully locking the box with the key.

'Let me out! Let me out!' shouted the angry mouse – but nobody would. 'I want to go and find adventures,' wept the mouse.

'Well, you've found one now,' said the teddy bear. 'It isn't every mouse that gets locked up in a moneybox. You'll just stay there till tomorrow, Mickey, and then Donald will come and let you out.'

All the toys went back to their games, and whom do you think they found sitting in the middle of the nursery hearth rug? Why, Tibby the cat! *Wasn't* it a good thing that Mickey was safely locked up in the moneybox?

Next morning Donald went to his daddy for his Saturday pennies. He had three, one for sweets, one for a toy and one for his moneybox He ran to the nursery shelf to take down his box.

'Squeak-eak-eak!' said Mickey the mouse, when he heard the penny come rattling in at the slit. 'It hit me on the nose. Squeak-eak-eak!'

'What's that squeaking noise?' wondered Donald, and he got his key and undid the box – and when he saw his pet mouse inside, you should have seen his astonishment!

'But however did you get there?' he cried. 'You're too big to get in at the slit! Someone must have unlocked the box and put you in, and then locked the box up again. What a very strange thing!'

He put the little mouse back into its cage, and shut the door. Mickey was *so* glad to be back. He had had quite enough adventure to last him for weeks – and when he saw Tibby the cat sitting on the hearth rug, he felt quite glad that the toy clown had locked him into the moneybox.

But Donald is puzzled to this day to know how Mickey got into his locked moneybox. Wasn't it a clever idea of the toy clown's?

How John Got His Ducklings

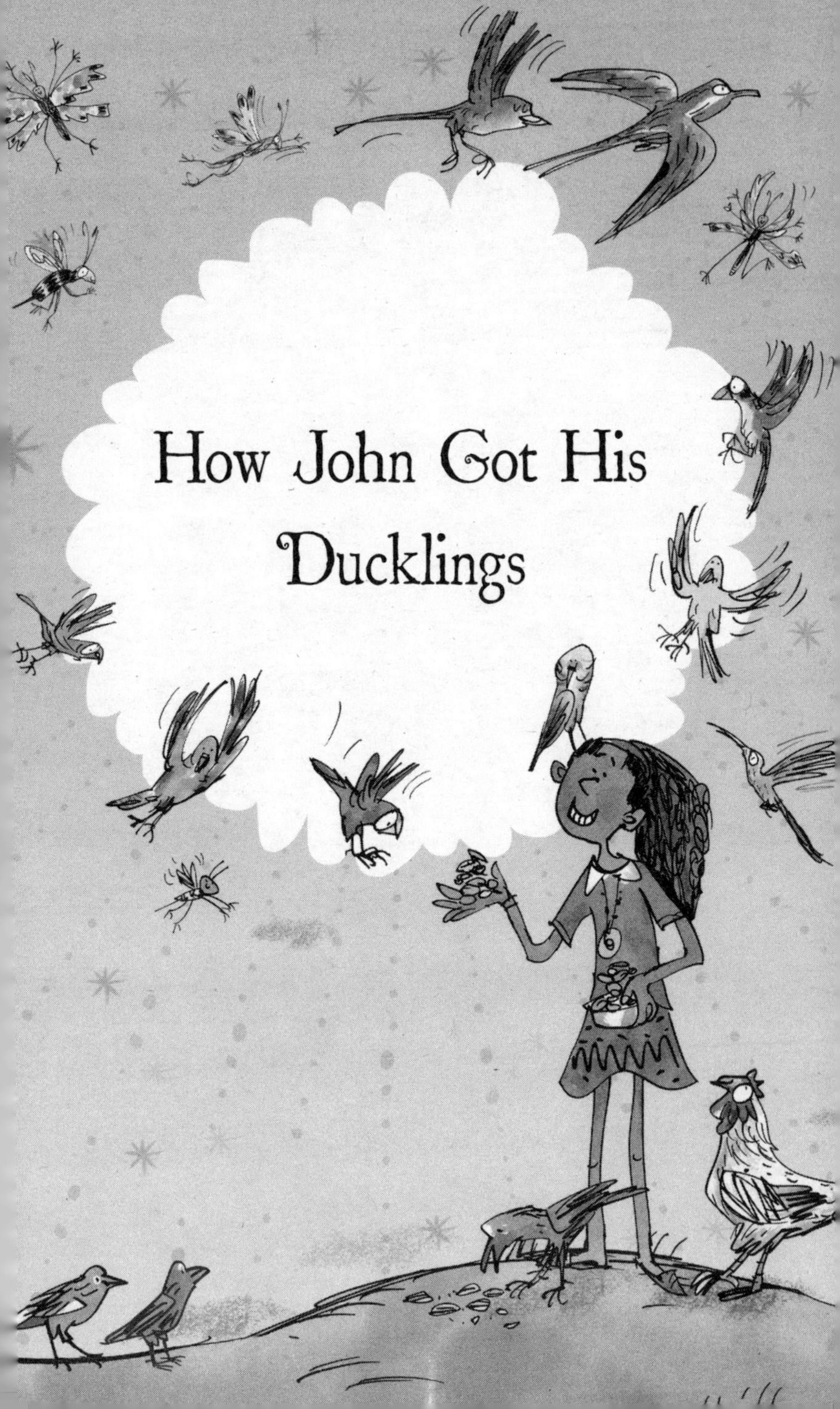

How John Got His Ducklings

JOHN LIVED on a farm, and he liked it very much. He loved old Dobbin the carthorse, Bessie the donkey and Daisy, Clover and Primrose the three brown-and-white cows. He loved the white sheep in the fields, and the brown hens and white ducks that wandered about everywhere.

Best of all he liked the baby animals and birds. He was always wanting some for his very, very own. But his father wouldn't let him have any.

'No, John,' he said. 'You're not old enough. You wouldn't look after them properly. You'd forget to feed them or something. Wait till you are old enough.'

'But, Daddy, I'm old enough now,' said John. 'I would feed them and water them well, Daddy, really I would. Just let me have two or three yellow chicks for my own, or some of those little yellow ducks. Do, Daddy.'

But Daddy shook his head, and John knew it was no use saying any more.

So he contented himself with trying to help Daddy feed the animals, and running after Jim, the yard man, when he went to make the pig meal or hen food. But all the same he longed and longed to have something that was really and truly his own.

One day Jim went to cart straw for the stables. John thought he would cart straw too. He had a little wooden cart and wooden horse. He could fill the cart with straw and then pull it along by dragging the horse after him. He could put the straw in the dog's kennel.

So he piled straw into his wooden cart. The straw was away in the field beyond the duck pond, and it was quite a distance from the dog's kennel. When John had filled the cart he picked up the string tied to his wooden horse's neck and began to pull it – but dear me, just as he reached the hawthorn hedge not far from the pond, the horse caught its wooden stand sharply against a stone and cracked it in half.

'Oh!' said John in dismay. 'It's broken! Poor old wooden Dobbin! I'll take you to Jim. Perhaps he can mend you for me tonight.'

He took the horse from the cart, and, leaving the cart of straw behind him, he ran off to find Jim.

'Yes, I'll mend it for you sometime,' said Jim. 'But not tonight.'

He took the horse from John. By that time it was dinnertime, and John had to run indoors to wash. He forgot all about the cart he had left out in the fields.

There it stood, all by itself, full of straw. Nobody saw it, for nobody went that way. It stayed there quite forgotten until one fine morning when a big white duck squeezed herself through the hawthorn hedge and waddled over to the cart to see what it was.

When she spied the straw inside, she jumped into the cart very clumsily and sat down. What a fine place to lay an egg! Ha, this was better than any place the other ducks had got! She laid a beautiful big greeny-grey egg there and then sat on it for a little while before she went back to the pond.

Each day the duck came to the little wooden cart that stood under the shelter of the hawthorn hedge, and laid a nice big egg there. Soon there were twelve, and the duck looked at them proudly.

She made up her mind to sit on them and keep them warm. So every morning very early, long before anyone was up to milk the cows, the duck waddled off from the pond and sat on her eggs. She just fitted the wooden cart nicely, and she liked the straw inside because it made such a nice nest for her eggs.

John waited and waited for Jim to mend his little wooden horse – and after some weeks, Jim did at last mend it. And then John had to hunt for his wooden cart! He had quite forgotten where he had left it.

He hunted here and he hunted there. Nobody had seen it, and it was a puzzle where to look for it!

'I say, John!' called Daddy. 'You might look out for ducks' eggs while you're hunting for your cart. I think one of the ducks has been laying away each day, and she may have a nest somewhere.'

'I'll look hard, Daddy,' said John.

'You can have the eggs for yourself if you find them,' said Daddy.

Oooh! If only John could find them! But he knew how clever ducks were at laying eggs in places he couldn't find or couldn't get at, so he hadn't much hope of finding a nest of them.

Suddenly he remembered where he had left his wooden cart. Of course! He had been carting straw like Jim when his horse had broken. He must have left his cart somewhere out in the field where the straw was.

Off he ran – and sure enough there was his little wooden cart by the hawthorn hedge, just where he had left it all those weeks ago. Hurray!

John ran to it – and when he reached it, he stood and stared – for there was something in his cart! It was a big, fat, white duck, sitting contentedly on the straw in his toy cart!

John looked and looked, and the duck looked back. She knew John and liked him – so she didn't mind when he slipped his hand under her and felt in the straw.

'Eggs!' said John. 'A whole nest of them! Oh, and Daddy said I might keep them if I found them! Oh, how lovely! I might have some ducklings of my own at last!'

He took hold of the shafts of the cart and gently wheeled it through the gap in the hedge to where Daddy was working near the pond.

'Daddy! Look!' called John. Daddy looked – and *how* surprised he was to see John with a cart in which a big white duck was sitting!

'She's got a whole lot of eggs!' said John. 'Can I have them, Daddy? I should think they will soon hatch into ducklings!'

'Well, well, well!' said Daddy, smiling. 'There's a find for you! Yes, you can have them, John, since you found them. But take your cart back to where you found it, or the duck won't go on sitting.'

So John took the cart back, and the duck said 'Quack', which meant 'Thank you', John was sure.

One day the eggs hatched into yellow ducklings, the fluffiest, prettiest little things you ever saw – twelve of them! They follow John about all day long!

Does he look after them well? Of course he does! He has never forgotten once to feed them or to give them water. Daddy says he will make a splendid farmer when he grows up.

'I shall always love ducklings best,' John says, 'because they were the first things I had for my very own. And I'll never, never give my little wooden cart away, because it was there I found the eggs!'

The Remarkable Tail

The Remarkable Tail

ONE DAY the toad who lived under the old mossy stone crawled out to have a drink from the water near by. He was a wise old fellow, and nobody knew how long he had lived under his stone. No one dared to take the hole he lived in, for it belonged to the toad.

As the toad slid into the water, a perky little creature swam up to him.

'Hallo, Toad! How are you?'

'Good morning,' said the toad, swimming away. 'And goodbye!'

'Ho! You think yourself very high and mighty, don't you?' said the long-tailed creature, swimming along by the toad. 'I've heard all about you – but *I* don't think you are very wonderful!'

The toad turned to look at this cheeky creature. It was a newt in his spring dress. He had a fine wavy crest all down his back, and a long, graceful tail. Underneath he shone brightly with a beautiful orange colour.

'Go away,' said the toad.

'But I want to talk like you,' said the newt. 'Why does everyone think you are so wise? You don't look it! I think you are an ugly creature! You have no graceful tail as I have! And look at my beautiful orange tummy!'

'I don't want to,' said the toad. 'It looks like one of those horrid-smelling toadstools that grow in the woods in autumn.'

'I do think you look odd without a tail!' said the cheeky newt. 'Why don't you try and grow one?'

'Why should I?' said the toad. 'I am a wise toad, not a foolish newt like you!'

With that he turned and swam to the edge of the

pond. He crawled out and went back to his stone, thinking angrily of the newt. *He will come to a bad end!* thought the old toad. *Foolish young creature!*

The newt was very proud of having talked to the toad. He told everyone about it. 'I showed him my tail, and my lovely orange colouring,' he said. 'And I waved my crest at him and told him he was an ugly fellow! He swam back to the bank feeling very sorry for himself, I can tell you! Oh, I am a grand fellow, I am! When I'm as old as that toad I shall be twice as wise as he is!'

The newt often used to leave the pond and go to the stone where the toad lived. This annoyed the toad, who liked to be alone. Besides, the newt liked flies for dinner, and was delighted to feast on caterpillars – and the toad liked these things very much too.

'Go away!' he said to the newt. 'You are a cheeky youngster, and will come to a bad end. You are foolish to leave the pond like this and come wandering up here. I am safe under my stone. You have no shelter and can easily be seen!'

'Fiddlesticks!' said the newt. 'I am no coward like you! Who will catch me, I should like to know? I am on the lookout for any rat, or snake or stoat!'

Sure enough, when the quiet rat came running up behind the newt, the little creature heard him, and at once slid through the grass to the water. Plop! He was in the pond at once!

Another time the grass snake glided up and the newt shot off just in time. The toad heard the splash as he leapt into the pond. The snake wondered whether to swim after him or not, but decided to look under the stone and see if anyone was hiding there. But when he saw the old toad he drew back his head hurriedly. He had once struck at a toad and tried to swallow him – and the creature had covered himself with such an evil-tasting liquid that the snake had spat him out in disgust. No! Toads were not good to eat.

'Didn't I tell you that I could always escape my

enemies?' said the newt, running up to the toad's stone again, as soon as the snake had gone. 'You are slow, Toad, but I am quick. You can only crawl – but I can run. Don't you think my tail looks extra well today? The crest goes all the way down to the end. I have been told that I am the prettiest creature in the pond.'

'Well, you are certainly the most talkative,' said the toad. 'I am tired of you. For the twentieth time, Newt, go away, and find someone who likes listening to you. I do NOT!'

'I shall stay here,' said the newt. 'It is nice and comfortable here, and the sun is warm.'

The toad said nothing more. He sat at the entrance to his hole and blinked. Then he saw something that made him stare upwards. A great bird was flying down to the pond. What a big bird it was! It flapped its huge wings so slowly, and trailed its long legs behind it.

A heron! thought the toad. *Ha! He is going to fish in the pond for frogs, newts or fish! He will see this silly newt – and that will be the end of him!*

But the toad was kind-hearted, and he called to the curled-up newt, 'Go back to the pond! The heron is coming!'

'I don't believe you!' said the newt. 'You are only saying that to get rid of me!'

The heron flew lower – and the newt suddenly saw the shadow of the great wings above him. In terror he tried to run away – but the heron landed beside him and then he picked up the newt by the tail. He was about to swallow him, when the toad called out loudly, 'Break off your tail! Break off your tail!'

The frightened newt wriggled and snapped his long, graceful tail right off. He left it in the heron's mouth and fell down into the water. He used his little feet to swim along, and disappeared into a hole in the bank, tailless, scared – but safe!

The heron said, 'Kronk!' in a deep voice, and flew off. The newt's tail was not much of a dinner – but the heron knew of another pond that was swarming with frogs!

The toad crept out from his stone and went to the pond. He slipped into it and swam about until he found the hole in which the newt was hidden.

'Are you safe?' he croaked.

'Yes – but I have lost my beautiful tail,' said the newt sadly. 'Still, I am grateful to you for telling me of that trick.'

'I saw a lizard play that trick once,' said the toad. 'Your tail will grow again.'

He swam off and went back to his hole.

'That newt needed a lesson,' he said to himself. 'Now he has got it. Perhaps he will be a wiser newt in future.'

The toad saw no more of the newt for many months – and then one day he saw him again outside his stone.

'Good day, Toad,' said the newt, in a humble voice. 'I have not come to worry you – only to say that my tail has grown again, though it is not nearly so nice as it was before – and I am wiser now, and no longer think I am the most wonderful creature in the pond.'

The toad crept out from under his stone and looked at the newt. Certainly his tail had grown – but what a stumpy one compared to his other!

'You may not be so beautiful now, but you are certainly nicer,' said the toad. 'Come and see me as often as you like. I think that we will be friends now!'

And now you may often see the newt talking to the toad by his stone. You will know him by his stumpy tail. Wasn't it lucky for him that the toad taught him the trick of breaking off his tail? No wonder he is grateful!

Goldie, the Cat Who Said Thank You

Goldie, the Cat Who Said Thank You

'JEAN!' CALLED Mother. 'I want you to go on an errand for me!'

'Where to?' asked Jean, running up.

'To Mrs Hunt at Home Farm,' said her mother. 'Fetch me six new-laid eggs, darling.'

'All right,' said Jean, and fetched her little egg basket. 'I won't be long, Mummy.'

Off she went, over the fields and across the little brown stream to Home Farm.

Mrs Hunt was feeding her chickens when Jean got to the farm. She smiled at the little girl.

'Good morning, my dear,' she said. 'Does your

mother want some of my nice eggs?'

'Yes, we would like six eggs, please,' answered Jean. 'Where's Philip?'

'Philip's round at the big barn,' said Mrs Hunt. 'He's got some fine kittens there, if you'd like to see them!'

'Yes, I would!' said Jean. 'I'll go now.'

She ran round to the big barn and went in. There she saw Philip, Mrs Hunt's son, bending over a litter of kittens lying in some hay.

'Hallo, Jean!' he said. 'Come and look at these! Two of them are real beauties!'

Jean bent over the kittens. Tibs, the mother cat, washed herself calmly and took no notice – she knew Philip and Jean would do no harm.

'They haven't got their eyes open yet,' said Philip. 'Aren't these two sweet? Their hair is long and silky already. They ought to be fine cats.'

'But why don't you like the little third one?' asked Jean. 'He looks quite a dear.'

'What! That ugly little sandy fellow!' said Philip

scornfully. 'He's not worth keeping!'

'But he can't help being that colour!' said Jean. 'What are you going to do with him?'

'I'll have to give him away,' answered Philip. 'Mummy will only let me keep two.'

'Oh, poor wee thing!' cried Jean. 'What a shame, just because he's not got long silky hair, like the others!'

'Well, you have him then,' said Philip. 'You haven't got a cat, have you?'

'No, I haven't. Oh, I wonder if Mummy would let me have him!' cried Jean, jumping up. 'I'll go and ask her about it this very minute!'

She ran to Mrs Hunt and took the eggs. Then, going as fast as she dared, for she was afraid of breaking the precious eggs, she hurried home again.

'Mummy!' she called. 'Here are the eggs. And oh, Mummy! Philip's got three kittens, and he's only allowed to keep two. The other will be given away if I don't have it! Can I have it, Mummy? Oh, please can I?'

'Oh, Jean dear!' said her mother. 'I really don't

think you can! I simply haven't any money at all to spare to pay for cat food!'

'How much does cat food cost?' asked Jean. 'Could I have the kitten if I give you the money that Great-Aunt Jane gives me every Saturday for running her errands for her?'

Mother looked at Jean and thought for a moment.

'Do you want that kitten very badly?' she asked, smiling. 'Is it worth that much to you?'

'Oh yes!' answered Jean.

'Well, you may have it,' said her mother. 'You can pay me half of your money every Saturday, and keep the rest yourself.'

'You darling!' squeaked Jean, and hugged her mother as hard as ever she could. 'Thank you.'

'Well, you can go and tell Philip,' said Mother. 'And you can fetch the kitten when it's old enough to leave its mother.'

Jean ran off, feeling most excited, and told Philip what she was going to do.

'All right,' he said. 'It's a good thing for that kitten you came along when you did! I hope that it will be a grateful kitten and will say thank you!'

'Don't be silly, Philip,' said Jean. 'Cats don't know how to say thank you.'

In a few weeks Jean fetched the kitten to her own home. It was a little tabby, thin and not very pretty, but Jean didn't mind about that at all.

'You're certainly worth half my money each week,' she said, hugging the kitten to her. 'And I'm going to buy a lovely red collar for you.'

The kitten loved Jean. It followed her about all over the place, and purred whenever it saw her. It played all sorts of tricks on her, and jumped at her feet as if they were a couple of scampering mice.

Jean loved the kitten, and when the little boy next door laughed at it, she told him he was horrid.

'You shouldn't laugh at the kitty,' she scolded. 'It will make him miserable!'

'Fiddlesticks! Kittens haven't any sense, as everyone

knows!' said the boy, laughing.

'This one has!' said Jean and took her kitten indoors without saying another word.

She couldn't think what to call him at first. Then, because he had fine golden whiskers, she called him Goldie.

He seemed to like his name very much, and always came scampering to Jean when she called him, wherever he happened to be.

'He's not at all a bad little kitten,' said Mother one day. 'He's growing a lovely strong, smooth coat, Jean. He may be quite a nice cat, after all!'

'Of course he will!' said Jean. 'I believe he will be beautiful, Mummy!'

One day Great-Aunt Jane asked Jean what she did with the money she got every week for running her errands on Saturday.

'I give Mummy half of it to help pay for Goldie's food,' said Jean. 'The rest I spend on all sorts of things.'

'Who's Goldie?' asked Great-Aunt Jane.

'He's my own cat,' said Jean. 'He's a perfect darling.'

She told Great-Aunt Jane all about how she came to have him.

'Dear me! That's very interesting!' said Great-Aunt Jane. 'I'm very fond of cats. I used to keep some beauties. You must bring your Goldie and let me see him next Saturday.'

'Perhaps you won't think he's very beautiful,' said Jean. 'Nobody seems to think much of him, except me.'

'Well, bring him, and I'll tell you exactly what I think,' said Great-Aunt Jane with a smile.

So the next Saturday Jean carried Goldie all the way to Great-Aunt Jane's. He had grown into a big cat, and his tail was very long. His eyes were amber green, and his whiskers were still very golden. He was heavy, but Jean didn't dare to put him down, just in case he ran away and got lost.

'Good morning, Aunt Jane,' she panted, when she reached her great-aunt's house at last. 'I'm sorry I'm late, but Goldie was so heavy.'

'So that's Goldie, is it?' said Great-Aunt Jane, taking him from Jean. She stroked him and he purred loudly. Then she gave him a saucer of creamy milk, and watched him while he drank it.

'What do you think of him?' asked Jean anxiously.

'Well, my dear, he's a real beauty!' said Great-Aunt Jane. 'You must surely have taken great care of him to make him so sturdy and sleek!'

'Oh, do you really think he's beautiful?' asked Jean in delight.

'Do you know what he is?' asked Great-Aunt Jane suddenly. 'He's a golden tabby, and one of the finest I ever saw! I had two once, but they weren't nearly as lovely as your Goldie!'

Jean could hardly believe her ears. She suddenly hugged Great-Aunt Jane, then she hugged Goldie, and then she hugged her great-aunt once more.

'Bless the child!' said Great-Aunt Jane. 'She thinks I'm a cat too, to have all the breath squeezed out of me! Now I've got an idea, Jean. Listen!'

'What?' asked Jean breathlessly.

'There's a cat show to be held here in a month's time,' said Great-Aunt Jane. 'We'll enter your Goldie in the golden tabby class, and see if he wins a prize!'

'Oh! Oh! Do let's!' squeaked Jean in delight, hugging her great-aunt again.

'Jean! Do let me breathe!' said Great-Aunt Jane. 'Well, if we do that you must keep Goldie very spick and span all month and brush him every day. You must see that he's fed well too. I will give you some money every week for him, so that Mummy won't be worried.'

'You are a perfect dear,' said Jean, hugging Goldie, instead of Great-Aunt Jane.

So it was all arranged. Great-Aunt Jane wrote to the cat show people and entered Goldie in the golden tabby class.

One day she gave Jean a big green ticket which had Goldie's name on it.

'Here you are,' she said. 'Next Saturday bring your

Goldie here, and we'll put his cat show ticket on him. Then we'll all go to the show, and see what happens!'

Jean was so excited. She brushed Goldie every day, and fed him well and regularly. Mother got quite excited too, when she heard about it all.

At last the cat show day came.

Mother and Great-Aunt Jane, Goldie and Jean, all went into the town hall, and found the place where Goldie was to sit that day.

Jean was so excited. Her knees kept shaking, so that she felt everyone must wonder what was the matter with her legs. When the judges came round to look at Goldie, she could hardly breathe.

And what do you think? Goldie won the first prize in the golden tabby class!

'He's a most beautifully shaped cat,' one of the judges said to Jean. 'And his colouring is lovely. Everything about him matches – his coat, his eyes and his whiskers! Here's the first prize rosette for you. Hang it up by him!'

Jean couldn't say a word. She took the rosette, and hung it up for everyone to see. Her mother and Great-Aunt Jane were pleased.

'I told you so. I told you so!' said Great-Aunt Jane, banging the floor with her stick.

And when Jean went to get Goldie's prize, she found it was a pound! She took Goldie up with her to get it, and everyone began to clap loudly.

But what Jean liked very nearly the best of all was when she carried Goldie over to Philip that evening.

'My word! What on earth is that rosette Goldie's got?' exclaimed Philip. 'First prize! I say, Jean, how lovely!'

'Isn't it glorious?' said Jean, hugging Goldie, while he purred as loudly as a tiger. 'And, oh Philip! This is his way of saying thank you for having looked after him!'

And Goldie purred more loudly than ever, for Jean was quite right. He had been meaning to say thank you!

Tie a Knot in His Tail

Tie a Knot in His Tail

'HEY, CLOCKWORK mouse!' called Molly, the doll's house doll. 'You said you'd come along and clean our windows yesterday, and you never came.'

'Oh, dear – I quite forgot!' said the little mouse. 'I'm so sorry.'

'Hey, clockwork mouse,' called the toy soldier, a minute later, 'did you look for that button that fell off my coat? You said you would.'

'Bother! I quite forgot!' said the mouse.

'He quite forgot!' repeated the teddy bear speaking in the clockwork mouse's squeaky little voice. 'He quite forgot! He never remembers anything. He doesn't even try to. He forgot to tidy up the brick box. He forgot to put the marbles away when he had rolled them all over the floor. He forgot to . . .'

'I'm sorry, I'm sorry!' said the little mouse. 'How can I remember things if I keep forgetting them? I do try, truly I do.'

'Tie a knot in his tail!' said Rabbit, with a grin. 'A nice big knot!'

'Why? Don't you dare to do such a thing!' cried the mouse in alarm. 'What a silly idea!'

'No, it isn't,' said the toy soldier. 'People tie knots in their hankies when they want to remind themselves of something – *you* haven't got a hanky – but you've got a nice long tail – so why not tie a knot in it to remind you of anything you want to remember? Easy!'

'But it might hurt to tie a knot in my tail?' said the mouse, sitting down hard on it.

'Oh no it won't,' said the sailor doll, entering into the fun. He pulled the mouse's tail out from beneath him, and very quickly tied a beautiful little knot in it, near the end. 'There you are – a knot in your tail!'

'But what's it *for*?' said the mouse, staring at it crossly.

'Well – let me think – you said you'd clean the little clockwork motorcar this morning,' said the sailor doll. 'And that knot is to remind you to do it. See? Every time you look at your tail you must say "Ah – I'm to clean the motorcar."'

'Oh, I see,' said the clockwork mouse, cheering up. 'It does seem a good idea, I must say. But can I untie the knot when I've remembered what it's for?'

'When you've remembered the job *and* done it!' said the teddy bear. 'Not before.'

'Why don't you go and clean the car *now*, this very minute?' asked the toy soldier. 'Then you can untie the knot very soon.'

'No. I want to have a little play,' said the mouse, and he ran off to roll the marbles about all over the floor. He loved doing that.

Rabbit called to him after a while. 'Hey, clockwork mouse, don't you forget to put those marbles away when you've finished playing with them. I keep falling all over them when I go walking round the playroom.'

'Tie a knot in his tail!' cried the teddy bear at once. 'Tie a knot in his tail. Then he'll remember! He'll have a knot to remind him to clean the car and a knot to remind him to put away the marbles!'

'But how shall I know which knot is which?' said the mouse as the toy soldier began to tie a second knot in his tail.

'Well, I'll tie a *third* knot in your tail to remind you that the first knot is for the motorcar and the second one is for the marbles,' said the toy soldier, with a loud giggle.

'No, don't do that. You'll muddle him,' said the teddy bear, so the toy soldier only tied one more knot instead of two.

Presently Big Doll got out of her cot and called to the little mouse. 'Hey, clockwork mouse, I lent you my little rug yesterday for you to cuddle into, because it was cold. Bring it back now, please.'

'I'm busy,' said the mouse, rolling another marble over the floor. 'Very busy. I'll bring back your rug later on, Big Doll.'

'You won't remember,' grumbled the doll.

'Tie a knot in his tail!' yelled all the toys again, and the toy soldier ran over to the mouse at once. He tied quite a big knot there, behind the other two. 'A big knot to remind you that it's Big Doll's rug,' he said. 'My goodness, your tail looks funny!'

'I don't think I like it,' said the mouse, looking round at his knotty tail. 'It's uncomfortable to sit on too. I won't have the knots in after all. Please untie them.'

'Not till you've done all the things the knots are to remind you of!' said the teddy bear firmly. 'Then we'll untie them.'

The clockwork mouse was cross. '*I'll* untie them then!' he said. But he couldn't. He simply couldn't. He ran to the sailor doll, who was a very kind fellow.

'Untie my knots. I don't like them any more,' he said.

'No. I'll untie them when you've remembered to do everything you promised to do,' said the sailor doll. 'If you do all the things straight away, I'll untie the knots in a very little while.'

The mouse ran off in a rage. His knotty tail knocked against the floor and made a funny noise. He didn't like it. Perhaps he had better do the little jobs he had promised, then the sailor doll would undo the horrid knots.

He looked at the first knot. Now, what was that there for? What had he promised to do? He couldn't remember. He just – simply – couldn't – remember!

He ran to the toy soldier. 'What's the first knot for? I can't remember.'

'Well! What's the good of putting knots in your tail if you don't remember why they're there!' said the toy soldier impatiently. 'Go away! I'm tired of you.

Keep the knots for the rest of your life!'

The mouse ran to the sailor doll. 'Tell me, do tell me, what are all these knots for?' he begged. 'I can't remember what I'm supposed to do for them.'

'No, I shan't tell you,' said the sailor doll. 'But I'll put another knot in, if you like, to remind you *not* to keep asking us to undo your tail till you've done the things you should!'

The clockwork mouse ran off with a squeal. He felt very unhappy. Suppose he never, never remembered what the knots were for? Goodness, he would never be able to go to sleep comfortably any more, with such a knotty tail.

'Hallo, Knotty!' said the teddy bear, as the mouse ran past him. 'Remembered your promises yet?'

'No. And *don't* call me Knotty,' said the mouse angrily. 'It's a horrid name.'

'It's a *good* name for you! said Rabbit. 'Knotty! Knotty, Knotty, Knotty! How does your tail feel now, Knotty?'

The mouse almost burst with rage. 'I'll never speak to you again!' he squealed.

'Good,' said Rabbit. 'I always said you talked too much. I say, toys – what shall we do when there's no more room in the mouse's tail for knots?'

'Tie knots in his whiskers!' shouted the teddy bear, and rolled over squealing with laughter at the idea.

Poor clockwork mouse – he really was very upset! He ran crying to the mouse hole where the real mice lived. He had a little friend there called Whiskers. He ran down the hole, calling for him.

He was soon telling Whiskers about his trouble. Whiskers wouldn't undo the knots. He said that he would have to use his teeth, and as they were very sharp, he might hurt the clockwork mouse.

'But why don't you remember what they're for and go and do everything?' he asked.

'Because I simply *can't* remember, you silly Whiskers!' wailed the clockwork mouse. 'Help me,

Whiskers, help me. Remember some jobs for me, please do.'

Whiskers remembered a great many, because he had so often heard the toys scolding the mouse for not doing what he had promised to do. He rattled off a lot of jobs in one breath.

'Clean out the engine trucks, find the little doll's brooch, clean the doll's house windows, put away the marbles, find where one of the bricks went to, take back the rug the Big Doll lent you, sweep the floor of the toy garage, tidy the bottles in the toy sweet shop, mend the . . .'

'Stop, stop!' cried the clockwork mouse. 'I only want to know the three things the knots are in my tail for, not a hundred silly jobs!'

'Oh, well, I don't know exactly which jobs the knots stand for,' said Whiskers. 'I only know *all* the things you said you would do, and haven't done. I'm afraid, clockwork mouse, that you'll have to do *all* the jobs, every one of them – then you are sure to do the ones the knots stand for, and you'll have them untied.'

The clockwork mouse ran back to the playroom, crying. How dreadful! He would have to work so very, very hard! But he hated his knotty tail so much that he felt there was nothing else to do!

He cleaned out the engine trucks at top speed. He hunted for the little doll's brooch and found it. He looked for all the marbles in every corner and put them neatly away. He found the missing brick and put it back in the brick box.

The toys watched him in amazement. What was all this sudden rushing about? Why was the clockwork mouse doing so very, very many things?

He took back the rug to Big Doll and then he swept the floor of the toy garage, and made such a dust that all the toys sneezed. He tidied the little bottles of sweets in the toy shop, and then he went to get a cloth to clean the doll's house windows. He had never been so busy in all his life before!

'Stop, clockwork mouse,' said the toy soldier at

last. 'You look tired out. Why are you working so hard all at once? There are only *three* knots in your tail, not a dozen!'

'I know. But I didn't remember what they were *for*,' said the poor little mouse, crying again. 'So I'm doing every single thing I can remember, hoping that three of them belong to the knots.'

'They do,' said the sailor doll, coming up. 'So I'll untie the knots. Keep still – there, they're all undone. Now for goodness' sake go and snuggle into the brick box and go to sleep. You're tired out, you silly little thing!'

'Don't tie any more knots in my tail,' begged the mouse. 'I'll remember all right without them. Really I will.'

'We'll see,' said the toy soldier. 'Now, do go to bed!'

The mouse ran off and curled up in a corner of the brick box. 'Goodnight, Knotty!' shouted Rabbit.

'Goodnight, Knotty!' called the teddy bear. 'Sleep well, Knotty!'

'I'm not knotty any more,' said the mouse sleepily. 'My knots are gone!'

But they still call him Knotty – and will you believe it, he's such a little forgetter that he's forgotten already why they call him by such a peculiar name. He'll have to go and ask Whiskers why, won't he?

It Takes All Sorts to Make a World

It Takes All Sorts to Make a World

ON ST Valentine's Day the birds all chose their mates. The robin chose the little hen he had been singing to for a long time. The chaffinch chose the bird he loved best, and the blackbird chose a dark-brown hen blackbird who thought his glossy black coat and orange beak were very beautiful.

They all met together to talk about the exciting business of nesting. I went to hear them, and what a lot they had to say!

'The best place to nest is in a tree,' said the blackbird. 'In a nice forking branch.'

'Nonsense!' said the little blue tit, excitedly. 'A tree

isn't safe, unless you build your nest in a hole. A hole is a marvellous place. I always build in a hole.'

'So do I,' said the starling. 'And by the way, blue tit, I wish you wouldn't always choose the hole *I* want.'

'Well I like *that*!' churred the blue tit angrily. 'Don't I have to send you away every time I find a nice hole to nest in? Don't you . . .'

'That's enough,' said the sparrow. 'It is plain there are not enough holes to go round. Now, a gutter is a fine place to build in. And there are many, many gutters, so . . .'

'No gutters for *me*, thank you!' said the little hedge sparrow. 'You town sparrows love to bring your children up in the gutter – but we hedge sparrows like a nice country bush.'

'The side of a cliff is better,' said a big gull. 'You know, there are lots of rocky ledges on a cliff and it's a good healthy place to bring up youngsters.'

'Well! I wouldn't dream of it!' said the little wren.

'I should be scared of my children falling off all the time. *I* like a cosy nest in a thatched roof.'

'Cosy! Who wants a *cosy* nest!' cried the lark. 'I've nested in the footprint of a big carthorse, and brought up my youngsters most comfortably. An open field is the best place.'

'No – a kettle or a tin or a saucepan – or even an old boot – those are fine places to nest,' said the little robin earnestly. 'Man is so friendly. It's nice to nest in something he has once used.'

'So *you* think!' said the owl. 'I wouldn't nest anywhere near man if I could help it.'

'Top of a tall tree!' cawed the rook.

'Hole in a riverbank!' cried the kingfisher.

'Inside a church tower!' cried the jackdaw.

'A field, an open field!' called the peewit.

'Excuse me,' I said, 'there's one bird, who is not here, who wouldn't agree with anything you are saying. He thinks it is best to build no nest at all! I mean the cuckoo!'

'The cuckoo! Don't talk to us about that bad bird!' cried the wagtail. 'He told his wife to put her egg into *my* nest last year – and I had to bring up a young cuckoo instead of my own children!'

'Maybe we are all wrong in our ideas about the best places to build a nest,' said the robin.

'No – you are all of you right!' I said. 'The more places you choose, the more room there is for all of you. Go and nest, little birds, and be happy!'

Will any of them nest in your garden? I hope so!

A Shock for Mr Meanie

A Shock for Mr Meanie

IT WAS cold weather, and Mr Meanie's old dog didn't like it. Mr Meanie wouldn't let him sleep in the house, so he had to sleep outside. He wouldn't have minded that at all if his kennel had been warm. But it wasn't.

There wasn't enough straw in it for one thing. And it faced the cold north wind for another. Old dog Trotter shivered and shook each night, but he couldn't go and curl up in a warm hedge because he was on a chain.

'Couldn't I have some more straw, Mr!' he would whine, when Mr Meanie went out in the morning. But

Mr Meanie had never been good at understanding dog language as some people are. So he didn't bring any more straw to old dog Trotter.

When the frost grew harder, Trotter's water froze. Trotter couldn't understand it. What had happened to his nice wet water? It wasn't wet any longer, it was dry and hard and cold. Trotter felt very thirsty indeed.

'Couldn't I have some water?' he whined to Mr Meanie the next day. But his master didn't understand a word, and never even noticed the frozen bowl.

One day he forgot to give Trotter his dinner. Trotter usually had a warm dinner, and how he looked forward to it. It warmed up his old bones and made him feel quite happy for a little while.

But that day Mr Meanie forgot all about his hot dinner, though old dog Trotter reminded him three times. He whined piteously, but Mr Meanie didn't understand. The old lady next door threw him a bone, and that was all Trotter got for two days.

That night the frost was harder than ever and the

north wind blew hard into Trotter's kennel. He had a round barrel for a kennel, so the wind got in easily. Trotter curled himself up at the very back, trying to pull a few wisps of old straw around him. But he couldn't possibly go to sleep because he was so cold, thirsty and hungry.

He shivered so much that his kennel shook and creaked. A small pixie, on her way to a meeting, heard the noise and came to see what it was.

'Trotter! Why are you shaking your kennel like that?' she asked. 'You are making such a noise.'

'I don't mean to,' said Trotter, glad to see someone who understood his language. 'I can't help it. I'm so cold that I shiver and my shivering shakes the kennel. Ooooh! I'm freezing!'

The pixie went inside. 'It's as cold in here as outside!' she said. She touched Trotter's body. 'Oh, you poor thing, you feel as cold as ice!'

'I'm so hungry too,' said poor Trotter. 'I keep thinking of hot gravy, and warm stew, and biscuits and bones, and things like that. And I'm thirsty. Something has happened to my water. It's gone hard and dry.'

'Why, it's frozen!' said the pixie. 'Oh, Trotter, I can't bear you to be so cold and hungry and thirsty. I really can't. Where's your master?'

'In bed, I expect,' said Trotter, shivering again. 'He doesn't understand my dog talk, Pixie. I keep telling him how cold and hungry I am. It wouldn't be so bad if he would turn my kennel away from this cold wind.'

'I'm going to help you,' said the pixie. 'I am on my way to a meeting, and I'm going to go there and tell everyone about you. And I'm going to bring them back here, and we'll soon shift your kennel round! I shan't be long!'

She ran off in the frosty moonlight. She found all her friends waiting for her at the meeting place, and she quickly told them about Trotter. They were sorry, and came back eagerly with her.

It was hard for such small folk to move the big, heavy barrel, even though Trotter got up and stood outside while they did it. But at last it was done. With scrapings and creakings it was swung to one side, so that the cold north wind no longer swept into it. Trotter crept in. It felt warmer already!

'Now we'll get you some straw, and some water and some food!' cried the pixie. Off she went with her friends, but there was no straw to be found anywhere. Nor was there any water, for every puddle was frozen hard. They could not find any food for Trotter and they came back, sad.

'Never mind,' said Trotter. 'I do really feel a bit warmer now I'm out of the wind.'

'Let's get into Mr Meanie's house,' said the pixie, to the others. 'There's sure to be warm bedding there and we can ask him for food and drink for Trotter.'

So they crept into the house. Mr Meanie was in bed, snoring so loudly that even the pixie's shouts did not wake him. She pulled and pinched him with her tiny hands, but he did not move.

She stood looking up at him. 'What a mean, unkind face he has!' she said to the others. 'I don't like him. I wish Trotter didn't belong to him. Look at all the lovely, warm blankets he has – and his poor dog didn't even have a handful of straw to keep him warm!'

'Well, let's take his blankets for Trotter!' cried one of her friends. 'We can tug and pull till we get them off!'

This seemed rather a joke to the pixies. So they began to tug and pull, and the blankets slid off Mr Meanie on to the floor. The pixie opened the front door, and the little folk dragged the warm blankets out to Trotter's cold kennel.

'Here you are, here you are!' they cried, and piled them all round the shivering dog. How delighted he was!

'I've never been so cosy in my life!' he said, burrowing into them. 'Now I shall be warm!'

The pixie ran back into the house to look for water.

But they could not turn the taps because they were too stiff for them. So they went to the larder and found a big jug of creamy milk.

'This will do!' said the pixie, and between them they managed to carry the heavy jug out into the yard. They emptied the milk into the bowl and called Trotter to come and drink.

He got out of the warm blankets and padded eagerly to the bowl. He lapped thirstily, and did not stop until he had finished every drop of milk.

'I never enjoyed a drink so much before!' he said. 'Never! Milk too – what a treat!'

The pixies forgot to take the empty jug back with them to the larder. They left it in the yard. They went back to the larder and looked for something for Trotter to eat.

'Here's a big meat pie,' said the pixie. 'And look, a joint of beef, already cooked! Let's take those to Trotter. He'll be pleased.'

Was Trotter pleased? He was much more than

pleased. He just simply couldn't believe his eyes and nose! He gobbled up the meat pie in a trice. Then he took the big joint of meat in his mouth and began to chew it.

'Oh, it's good, it's good!' he cried. 'Excuse my talking with my mouth full, but I can't help it. It's so good!'

A cock crowed in a nearby yard. 'We must go,' said the little folk. 'Goodbye, Trotter. We'll come and see if you are warm, and have something to eat and drink, tomorrow night. We won't forget you.'

They went off, leaving Trotter to finish the joint. Then the happy dog crept back into his warm blankets, and snuggled down in them, sleeping warm and cosy for the first night in weeks.

Now, the pixies had left the front door of Mr Meanie's cottage wide open. The wind swept in. His bedroom door was open too, and as he had no blankets over him he soon began to feel cold.

He was so cold that he stopped snoring and woke

up. He reached out for his blankets, which he thought must have slipped down. He couldn't feel them anywhere. He sat up and put on the light.

'I suppose my blankets are on the floor,' he said to himself. But they weren't. Mr Meanie looked everywhere, feeling most astonished. 'Where have they gone?' he kept saying. 'Brrrr! How cold it is! Where can that freezing wind be coming from?'

He thought he would get up and go downstairs to heat himself some milk. Then perhaps he would feel warm again. And maybe a slice of meat pie would make him feel better too.

He was astonished to find the front door wide open. 'Can thieves have been in and taken my blankets?' he wondered. 'My, how cold I am! Where's that jug of milk? I'll heat it up.'

But the big jug of milk wasn't there. Nor was the meat pie! And the big joint was gone too. Mr Meanie stared round the larder in great dismay.

'Thieves and robbers! Blankets gone – jug of milk

gone – and meat pie and joint gone! What am I to do? I shall freeze in bed, and tomorrow I shall have no food but a loaf of bread!'

There was nothing to be done but to go back to bed hungry, thirsty and cold. He wrapped his old coat round him, but that didn't warm him very much. And then the thought of old dog Trotter slid into Mr Meanie's mind.

Trotter hadn't even an old coat to keep him warm. Nor a handful of straw. And how cold that wind must be tonight, outside in the yard!

Mr Meanie half thought of going out into the yard and calling Trotter into the house. But he didn't.

The next morning he went out to see Trotter. Imagine his surprise when he found the old dog curled up in blankets – the blankets from his bed!

And there, beside the kennel, was the empty milk jug – and not far off was the empty meat pie dish – and dear me, was that the bone from the joint of meat? Yes, it was!

Mr Meanie stared and stared. He thought hard. It wasn't burglars that had come in last night. It couldn't have been Trotter himself, for he was on a chain. It couldn't possibly have been the policeman because he would have woken up Mr Meanie, and told him to look after his dog himself.

And somebody had shifted the kennel round so that it was now out of the wind. Mr Meanie began to feel very uncomfortable.

Who was it, that came into his house at night, and took his blankets, his milk and his food, and gave them to his dog? He felt ashamed too when he remembered that Trotter had no warm straw, and that he had forgotten to give him water and food.

'I must have my blankets back,' he said to Trotter. 'They're my only ones.' He took them away – but he slipped Trotter off his chain, so the dog was able to run about and keep himself nice and warm.

When he came back from his run he found that there was fresh water in his bowl, and biscuits mixed with hot gravy in his dish. Oh, good, good, good! Trotter wagged his tail, and gave Mr Meanie's hand a lick. Like all dogs, he was very forgiving indeed.

Another surprise awaited Trotter when he got into his kennel. It was filled with good, fresh straw, warm and cosy. 'Ha! This is even better than blankets!' said Trotter to himself, and began to make himself a kind of den in the middle of the straw.

'Trotter,' said Mr Meanie to his old dog, 'Trotter, listen to me. I don't know who it was that fed you last night, or gave you my blankets. But you must ask them not to do it again, because I'm ashamed of forgetting you, and I never will again. Do you understand, old dog?'

Of course Trotter understood. He wagged his tail hard, licked his master's hand, and gave a few joyful barks. And dear me, for once Mr Meanie understood dog talk, and smiled. I don't think he will forget old dog Trotter again, do you? And I shan't forget *my* dog either, on a cold and frosty night!

A Ride on a Horse

A Ride on a Horse

THE HORSES at Apple-Tree Farm were lovely. There were six enormous carthorses with long, thick manes and tails, and big, shaggy hooves. Sometimes when he awoke in the early morning Bobby could hear them going out to work.

Clippity-clop, clippity-clop, went their big feet as they walked slowly through the farmyard or up the lane. It was a lovely noise.

Besides the carthorses was a strong little pony that Uncle Jack rode. His name was Bonny. He sometimes pulled the smaller farm carts, but he didn't like that much. He liked to be ridden all over the farm.

'In summer all the horses live out in the fields,' said Jenny to Bobby. 'But when it gets really cold we put them into their stables at night.'

Bobby liked the stables. They smelt of horse, they were rather dark, and straw and hay were all over the place. Sometimes he pretended *he* was a horse, and went to stand in a stall, with his head over a manger of hay. He kicked with his heels on the floor, stamping like a horse.

He even neighed one day, and two of the dogs, one of the cats and three hens came to look in at the door to see what kind of a new horse the farmer had brought to his stable.

Once the cowman took a farm cart up into the field where Sam, the shepherd, was. He was taking some hurdles to him. He saw Bobby and beckoned to him.

'You come and sit beside me,' he shouted. 'And maybe I'll let you hold the reins for a bit.'

Bobby thought that would be rather a grand thing to do. So he climbed up on to the cart and took his place beside the cowman. 'Thank you, Jim,' he said. Jim solemnly handed him the reins.

'Oh, but I don't know *how* to drive!' said Bobby in alarm.

'Chestnut won't mind,' said Jim, with a very broad grin. 'She knows the way, so she does. No matter if you pull the reins the wrong way, she'll go right. You see if she doesn't.'

Well, Chestnut certainly went the right way, though whether it was because Bobby did hold the reins right or not, he didn't know. Anyway, it was lovely to be high up on the driving seat, holding the slippery leather reins, and feeling the pull of Chestnut's head as he went up the hill.

'I feel very grand,' Bobby said to Jim. 'I always wanted to drive a horse. I wish you'd let me do this again.'

'Hop up on my cart whenever you see me coming then,' said Jim. 'Old Chestnut won't mind!'

It was that very evening that Bobby rode on a

horse's back for the first time. He met his uncle coming down the lane, leading the great carthorse, Clopper.

'Hey, Bobby!' called his uncle. 'Come along here.' And when the little boy ran up, Uncle Jack suddenly lifted him high in the air – and bump, there he was on Clopper's broad back!

'Oooh!' said Bobby, surprised, half frightened and excited. 'Ooooh, Uncle! I'm up very high!'

'Gee-up, Clopper, old boy,' said Uncle Jack, and Clopper began walking off up the lane. Bobby almost fell off!

But somehow he hung on, bumping this way and that as Clopper plodded on. He smiled down at his uncle. 'It's fine,' he said. 'I like it. Let go of me, Uncle. I'll stay on all right.'

And when Peter and Jenny came running to meet their father, they *were* surprised to see him on Clopper's back. Bobby did have a lovely time, didn't he!

Where's the Kitten?

Where's the Kitten?

'WHERE'S THE kitten? Has anyone seen Sandy?' called Mummy. 'Denis, have you?'

'No. I haven't seen him for ages,' said Denis, looking up from his book.

'Mollie, have *you* seen the kitten?'

'No, I haven't,' said Mollie. 'He was playing about when I was tidying my doll's house, patting the tiny doll's house dolls and sniffing at them – but I haven't seen him since. I've been cleaning my bicycle.'

'Then where has he gone?' said Mummy, worried. 'He's too little to go off by himself. Oh, dear – I do hope he hasn't squeezed through the hedge into the garden next door! The dog there might pounce on him.'

'Well, *I* hope he hasn't run out into the road,' said Denis, getting up. 'There are so many cars going up and down. I'll go and look for him.'

He went out into the front garden and called loudly. 'Sandy, Sandy, Sandy! Where are you?'

But there was no funny little mew to be heard. Then Denis went to look through the hedge between his garden and the next. 'Sandy, Sandy!' he called. But the only answer he had was a 'wuff-wuff-wuff' from the dog there. He came running up to the hedge, wagging his tail. 'Well – Sandy can't be with *you*, that's certain!' said Denis. 'Wherever has the little thing gone?'

Mummy hunted, Mollie looked everywhere and Denis called and called. He even went into the garden shed to see if Sandy had crept in there. He was a most inquisitive kitten, and got into all kinds of strange places.

'Well, he's gone,' said Mummy at last. 'I think I'd

better ring up the police. Someone might have found him and taken him to the police station to wait till his owner reported him lost.'

'Goodness – he'd be very scared,' said Mollie. 'Wait, Mummy – he might be up a chimney. Don't you remember how our old cat once climbed up the dining room chimney and got stuck? We *couldn't* think where the mewing came from.'

So what did the children do but bend down at every fireplace and call up the chimney there. 'Sandy, Sandy, Sandy! Where are you?'

But still there was no mew to be heard. They gave up at last and Mummy telephoned the police station. 'We've lost our little sandy kitten. Has anyone reported finding one – or brought one in?'

'No, Madam. I'm sorry, but we've heard nothing about a kitten,' said a deep voice at the other end. 'We've got a dog in though – a little spaniel.'

'No – that's no good,' said Mummy. 'It's our kitten we want. Please let us know if one is brought in.'

She put down the receiver. 'No news,' she said.

'Oh Mummy,' said Mollie, almost in tears. 'I love him. He's such a funny, playful little fellow. I do wish he'd come back.'

'If only we could hear his little mew,' said Denis – and just at that very moment they heard it!

'Mew-ew-ew!'

'There – that's Sandy!' cried Mollie. 'Where is he? It sounded as if the mew came from the playroom!'

They all rushed there and listened. 'Sandy!' called Mummy. 'Mew-ew-ew!' came the answer. Where *was* the kitten? Where did the mew come from? They all began to hunt about the room, looking under the chest and under the divan, and behind the play box, calling all the time.

'This is silly,' said Mummy, at last. 'He *must* be in this room because we can hear his mew so well. Let's listen again.'

So they listened. 'Mew-ew-ew!' they heard, and Mummy pointed over to the window. 'It sounded as if it came from there,' she said.

'But there's nothing there except my doll's house!' said Mollie. And then she gave a little scream and pointed to it.

'Look, Mummy; look, Denis – look who's peeping out of the downstairs window of my doll's house!'

They all looked – and how they laughed! A little furry face peered at them, a face with big eyes and long whiskers – the kitten!

'Oh, Sandy – you must have squeezed in at the little front door to see if the house was all right for you to live in!' cried Mollie in delight. 'But you're too big, you really are.'

She opened the whole front of the house and out ran the kitten, leaping about in joy. Mollie picked him up. 'You funny little thing! Did you *really* want to live there – or did you just go visiting the tiny dolls you played with this morning?'

'Well, thank goodness we've found him,' said Mummy. 'Little rascal. Whatever will he do next?'

'Mew-ew-ew!' said the kitten. He knew what he *wanted* to do next – eat his dinner!

The Poor Pink Pig

The Poor Pink Pig

ONCE UPON a time there was a fat pink pig who belonged to Mother Winkle. Mother Winkle was half a witch and she sometimes made spells, but she didn't really know very much about them, and so they often went wrong.

The pig was called Acorn, and Mother Winkle often used to call him into the kitchen to help her with her spells. She hadn't a green-eyed black cat to help her, as most witches have – she couldn't afford one, for they were very expensive to buy. But Acorn the pink pig did quite well instead.

Acorn hated having to help Mother Winkle. The

spells smelt funny, and you never knew when green or yellow smoke would suddenly appear, or flames jump out of nothing. So he used to try to hide when he knew Mother Winkle was doing magic. It wasn't any good though – Mother Winkle always found him. He was too big to hide himself properly.

One day Mother Winkle shooed him into the kitchen to help her to do a new spell. Someone had given her a spell for magic cakes, and she wanted to make some. But to do that she had to get Acorn to stand in the middle of a circle of chalk while she stood outside and sang a lot of magic words.

Acorn didn't want to help, but he had to. He stood there in the middle of the chalk circle, looking very miserable. Mother Winkle stood outside with her magic stick and book, and then she began to recite enchanted words in a sing-song voice.

In two minutes, to Acorn's enormous surprise, a great many small currant cakes suddenly appeared inside the chalk circle, just by him.

There they were, smelling new-baked and most delicious. Acorn's mouth watered and his nose twitched. How he longed to sniff at one of those cakes, but he didn't dare move while the magic was going on.

Just as Mother Winkle put her book down to go and fetch a plate for the magic cakes, a knock came at the door.

'Bother! That's the butcher!' said Mother Winkle, and went to the door, leaving Acorn and the cakes alone in the circle.

Well, that was too much for Acorn. As soon as Mother Winkle's back was turned he sniffed at a cake, and it smelt so good he ate it. My goodness me, it tasted good too! Acorn ate another – and another – and another! In fact, he had eaten nearly all of them when Mother Winkle came back!

And then Acorn noticed something very, very strange. Mother Winkle looked enormous! Simply *enormous*! He couldn't make it out. He looked round the room – and squealed in surprise. The chairs and the tables were enormous too!

Those magic cakes had a spell in them to make anyone who ate them grow much smaller! Acorn had eaten a lot and he was now very tiny. Each cake had made him half his size!

Mother Winkle stared at him in amazement, and then she stamped her foot in anger.

'Oh, you silly, greedy pig! You've eaten nearly all my magic cakes! You wicked creature! Wait till I make you your right size again, and I'll turn you into bacon!'

Acorn was so frightened that he leapt out of the chalk circle and ran into a corner. Mother Winkle ran after him – and then the little pig discovered that it was much easier to hide himself now he was tiny. He squeezed into a mouse hole and stood quite still there. Mother Winkle poked here and there under the chairs but she couldn't find him anywhere.

Acorn squeezed himself still further back in the

mouse hole – and found himself against something warm and soft.

'Hallo, hallo!' said a squeaky voice. 'Who are you?'

Acorn turned and saw a little brown mouse with bright black eyes.

'I hope I'm not in your way,' he said politely. 'But the truth is I'm trying to hide from that horrid person Mother Winkle. She is going to turn me into bacon.'

'Dear, dear!' said the mouse, shaking his head in dismay. 'I'm sorry for you, I really am. She is not a nice person. She is mean. She never leaves a single crumb out for me or my family. Why don't you run away?'

'That's a good idea!' said Acorn in delight. 'Why should I ever go back? Oh, but, Mouse – there's one thing I had forgotten – I'm too tiny. Who will make me a big, proper pig again, if I don't go back to Mother Winkle?'

'No one will,' said the mouse cheerfully. 'But why do you want to be a big, proper pig? It's much nicer to be small. I've been small all my life and it suits me very well. You can hide beautifully, and creep anywhere you like. I should keep small if I were you.'

Acorn thought about it, and he decided that the mouse was right. It would be nice to be small.

'But I must find a home somewhere,' he said to the mouse. 'I must belong to someone.'

'Well, creep through my hole,' said the mouse. 'I'll show you where it goes. It leads to a farm, and you can ask the farmer's wife if she will keep you for her own pig. She is very kind to all animals. I expect she will let you live on her farm.'

So Acorn followed the kind little mouse through the long tunnel, and at last came up into a field. The mouse poked his head out to see if any of the cats were about, but none was to be seen.

'There's the farmer's wife, look!' whispered the mouse. 'Feeding her chickens – do you see? Go and ask her now.'

Acorn said goodbye to the mouse and hurried over to the farmer's wife. He squeaked at her from the ground and she suddenly saw him among her hens, looking very small indeed, tinier than the tiniest chick. She picked him up in astonishment.

'Will you give me a home?' squeaked Acorn. 'I have run away, and I want a new home.'

The farmer's wife laughed and shook her head.

'You funny little creature!' she said. 'You wouldn't be any good to me! You're too small! No, no you must go somewhere else!'

Acorn scampered away. He was sad. Where should he go now? He wandered on and on and at last came to a hillside where sheep, looking as large as elephants, were all busily eating the grass.

I'd like to live out here on the hillside, thought Acorn. *There's plenty of sunshine, and the sheep wouldn't take any notice of me. I'll go and ask the shepherd if he'll have me.*

So he went to where the shepherd was sitting on the grass, looking at the sky to see if rain was coming.

'Will you have me for your own?' squeaked the pig to the surprised shepherd. 'I'm a pig run away from home. I'm a real pig, but very small.'

The shepherd threw back his head and laughed.

'Who wants a tiny pig like you!' he said. 'You're no use to anyone. My dogs would smell you out and nibble you. Go away while there's time.'

The poor pink pig scampered off in a hurry, looking behind him to see if the sheepdogs were coming. He went on until he came to a goose girl, taking her geese on to the common. He ran up to her and tugged at the lace in her shoe.

'Let me be your pig!' he squealed. 'Let me live with your geese!'

The goose girl looked at him in astonishment.

'But what use are you?' she asked. 'Such a little thing as you are! Who wants a pig as tiny as you!'

The geese saw the tiny pig and began to hiss and cackle. They crowded round Acorn and he was frightened. He slipped between their yellow legs and ran off as fast as he could.

He hid himself all day, afraid of cats, dogs and

geese. When night came he set out once more, and soon came to a big house. He squeezed himself under the door and went in. The first room he came to was full of toys. There were dolls on a shelf, a ball on the floor, a clockwork engine in a cupboard with soldiers and a kite, and, just by the wall, a big Noah's ark.

Everyone was surprised to see the pink pig.

'Are you a toy?' asked the biggest doll.

'No, I'm a proper pig, but very small,' said the pig.

He told the toys all his adventures, and they were sorry for him. All the animals in the Noah's ark came out to look at him. There were two elephants, two bears, two lions, two tigers, two cows, two goats, two chickens, two ducks – in fact, two of everything.

No – not quite two of everything, after all. There was only one pig, a little black one. He ran over to Acorn and had a good look at him.

'Oh!' he said. 'I really thought at first that you were the other Noah's ark pig come back again. You know, he was left out of the ark one day, on the carpet – and when the housemaid swept up the next morning, she swept the little pig into her dustpan, and we never saw him again.'

'We think he must have been put into the dustbin with the rubbish and taken away,' said the biggest doll sadly. 'We miss him very much. You are rather like him.'

'I am very lonely without him,' said the Noah's ark pig. 'I suppose, little live pig, you wouldn't like to be a toy pig and live with us in the ark? We have great fun, for the children often take us out and walk us all round the floor. You would be well taken care of too, and we would all be friends with you.'

Well, you can imagine how delighted Acorn was! He rubbed his nose against the pig's nose and squealed for joy.

'Of course I'll live with you!' he cried. 'I'd love to! I don't want to be big any more. I like being little. And oh, it will be such fun living with so many animals. But, little pig, are you sure the lions and bears won't eat me?'

'Oh goodness me, no!' said the Noah's ark pig. 'They are made of wood. They are not alive like you. You will have to pretend to be made of wood too, when the children play with us.'

'Oh, I can easily do that!' said Acorn. He climbed back into the ark with all the others, and settled down for the night. He was so pleased to have found such a nice home. The ark was warm and comfortable, and the other animals were friendly and jolly. He was very happy.

But when the children, Anne and Margaret, played with their Noah's ark animals the next day, how surprised they were!

'Margaret! Here's another little pig instead of the one we lost!' cried Anne, picking up Acorn. 'Oh, isn't he nice and fat! He looks so real too. I wonder who put him there.'

Nobody knew. Mother didn't know, nor did

Father. Granny shook her head and so did Jane the housemaid. Nobody knew at all. You can't think how puzzled they all were!

Acorn still lives in the Noah's ark – and I'd love to tell Anne and Margaret how he got there, wouldn't you?

Here You Are, Squirrel!

Here You Are, Squirrel!

'WHAT *IS* Paul doing out in the garden on a day like this?' said Mother, one autumn day. 'Look at him there, scribbling something down in a notebook. What *is* he doing?'

Anne went to the window. 'There's a squirrel there too, Mother,' she said. 'Isn't he lovely with his big curling tail? Perhaps Paul is drawing him?'

They asked Paul when he came in, damp with the misty drizzle outside. He laughed.

'No. I'm not drawing him. You know I'm no good at that. I'm just watching the squirrel and seeing where he hides his nuts – and as we've got two or three in our own garden, it's easy for me!'

'I bet you'll be the only one who has a list of the squirrel's hidey-holes!' said Anne. 'Read us what you've put.'

'Well, it's not much,' said Paul. 'He put two acorns at the bottom of the oak tree in a little hole under a root. And he put some hazelnuts in the little ditch and covered them with damp leaves. And he tucked a chestnut or two into the hollow log. I'm going to add to the list tomorrow.'

'Goodness – do you suppose he'll remember all his hiding places when he comes out on a warm day in winter, feeling hungry?' asked Anne.

'I don't know. That's one of the things I hope to find out,' said Paul.

He went out again the next day, but when he came back, he looked upset. 'I've dropped my lovely silver pen somewhere,' he said. 'I've looked everywhere in the garden but I can't find it.'

'I'll help you,' said Anne, but although the two of

them looked in every corner they couldn't find it.

'Why did I take it out just to make notes on squirrels?' groaned Paul. 'I could just as well have used my school one! Blow – Daddy *will* be annoyed with me. He gave it to me for my birthday.'

The squirrels disappeared soon after that because cold, frosty weather came in, which they didn't like. 'They are all fast asleep in their nests,' said Paul. 'Well – the autumn's getting on now – December will soon be here – and Christmas time!'

November was at an end. December came in and was very cold. No squirrels scampered about anywhere in the woods or garden – but as January drew near a sudden warm spell came. The sun shone down all day, and a warm wind blew. The squirrels awoke and peered out of their trees.

'Nice and warm!' they chattered. 'Let's find our nuts. We're hungry!'

And, to Paul's delight, he saw the squirrel he knew so well back in his garden again in the warm sunshine.

He scrabbled here and he scrabbled there with busy little paws. Oh for a nice juicy nut! Oh for an acorn to nibble!

Paul laughed. 'There! I thought you wouldn't remember your hidey-holes, squirrel. Wait while I get my nature notebook and I'll soon tell you where they are.'

Soon he was out in the garden, calling to the squirrel again. 'Here you are, squirrel! Here's one hidey-hole at the bottom of this oak tree. You'll find two acorns there!'

Paul scrabbled a little with his hands and the squirrel watched. Then the lovely little thing bounded over and began to scrape in the earth there himself. He had remembered! He pulled out the two acorns.

'Do you want a hazelnut, too?' asked Paul. 'Well, here you are, squirrel – in this little ditch covered over with damp leaves. Don't you remember?'

The squirrel bounded over and uncovered the nuts. He scampered up on a bough and chattered away to the boy down below just as if he really was talking to him!

He had a good meal and then bounded down again. Paul called out to him. 'Are you still hungry? Well, I'll tell you another hidey-hole.'

But the squirrel didn't listen. He went to the foot of a big bare plane tree and began to scuffle about in the mass of dead leaves beneath it. Paul went slowly up to him, wondering if he had hidden nuts there too. Something bright suddenly glinted, as the squirrel scuffled the leaves here and there. Paul wondered what it was.

Then he suddenly knew. 'My silver pen! It is, it is! I must have dropped it there and the plane tree covered it up with a thick carpet of leaves! Oh, *thank* you, little squirrel! You've found it for me!'

The squirrel made a chattering noise again and leapt up the tree, then bounded across to another and was gone. Paul rushed indoors.

'Mother! Anne! I found the hidey-holes for the

squirrel – and look what he found *me* – my silver pen! I'm going to write out the whole story in my nature book!'

Well, he did – and his teacher sent it to me to read. I thought it was much too good a story to waste, so here it is!

Paul wants to know one thing. Did the squirrel *mean* to find his pen for him or not? Paul and Anne say yes, yes, yes! What do *you* say?

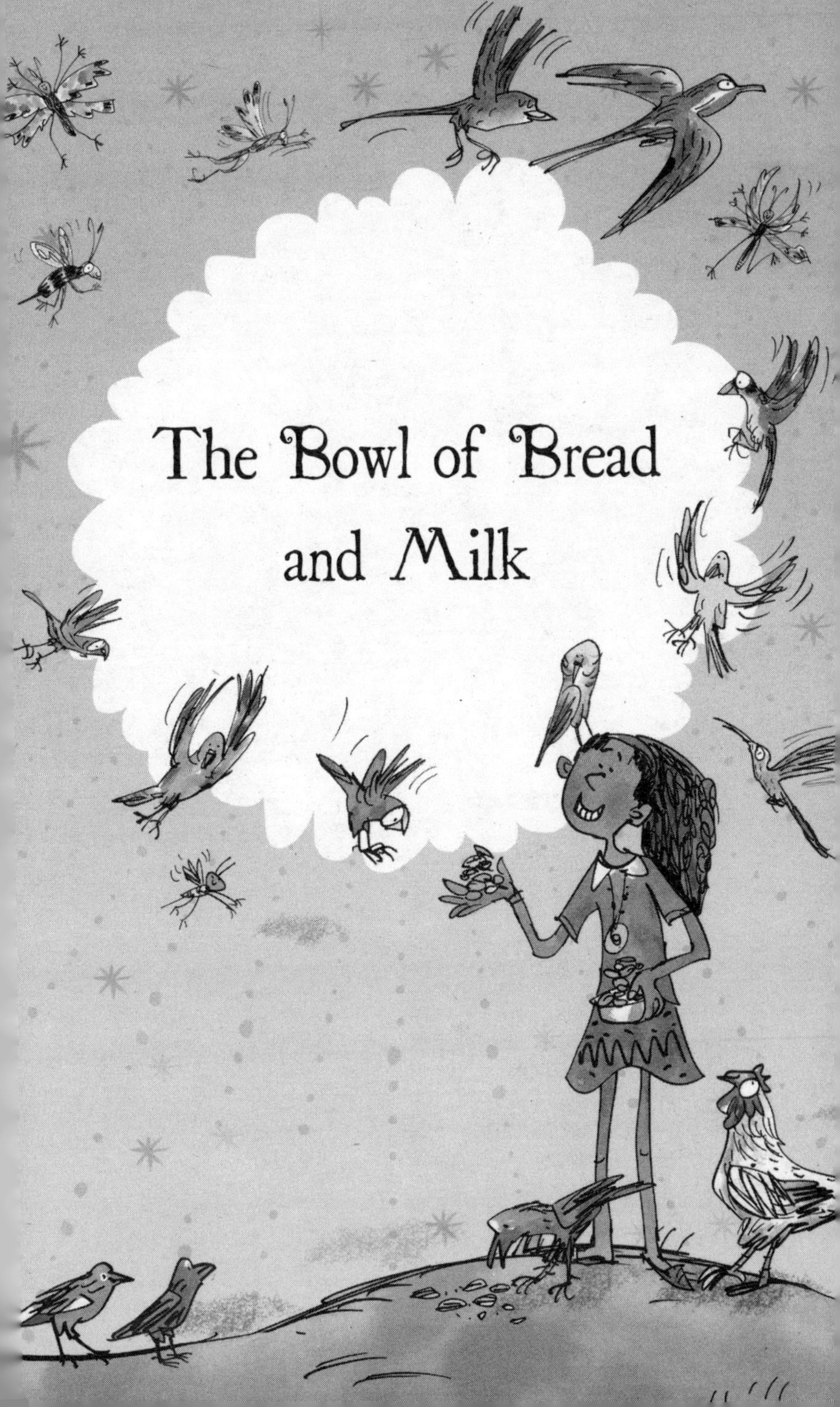

The Bowl of Bread and Milk

The Bowl of Bread and Milk

SOMEONE HAD put a bowl of bread and milk out into the garden. Little Angelina Brown wouldn't eat her breakfast, so it had been taken away from her, and put outside.

The blackbird saw it first, and cocked his head on one side. '*Tirrtoo!*' he sang. 'What a lovely feast!' and he flew down to have some.

Then the tiny mouse who lived under the tool shed smelt it, and popped his head out. 'Squeak!' he said. 'What a lovely feast!' and he ran over to the bowl.

Then who should come scuttling by but the hedgehog who lived in the ditch at the bottom of the garden. He suddenly saw the bread and milk and he stood still in delight. 'Ooh!' he said. 'What a lovely feast!' He ran over to the bowl, and there he met the blackbird and the mouse.

'Go away!' cried the blackbird, pecking the mouse with his strong, yellow beak. 'This is my bread and milk!'

'You go away!' squeaked the mouse angrily. 'I'm sure I saw this first. It's mine, you greedy blackbird!'

'It's not yours or the blackbird's,' said the hedgehog, putting his snout over the edge of the bowl. 'It's mine, so go away, both of you. I am very hungry this morning, so I shall finish this all up.'

Then the blackbird made an angry noise, and flew at him. He pecked him on the nose, and the hedgehog fell over on to the mouse, pricking him with his spines. The mouse squeaked in fright and nibbled one of the feathers in the blackbird's tail.

'Go away!' shouted the blackbird. 'This is my bread and milk!'

'Go away!' cried the hedgehog. 'This is my bread and milk!'

'Go away!' squeaked the mouse. 'This is my bread and milk!'

But none of them would go away, and they chased each other all round the bowl, making a most tremendous noise.

Now not very far away, on top of the garden wall, was Whiskers, the big black cat. He was fast asleep in the warm sunshine, but soon the loud noise made by the blackbird, the mouse and the hedgehog woke him up with a start. He sat up and looked around.

Then he saw the bowl of bread and milk and the three quarrelsome creatures fighting for it. He got up and stretched himself. Then he jumped down from the wall and made his way slowly towards the bread and milk.

The blackbird suddenly saw him and gave a squawk of fright. He flew away into a nearby tree. Then the mouse saw him, and squeaked in terror. He ran away to his hole and hid himself there in safety. Then the hedgehog caught sight of the cat too, and at once curled himself up into a spiky ball.

The cat took no notice of any of them. He went to the bowl and sniffed at it. Then he gave a purr of contentment and began to lap up the milk and eat the bread quickly, for he was very hungry. After that he sat down and carefully washed himself all over, not forgetting behind his ears, for he was a very clean cat. Then he went back to his place on the wall, lay down and fell fast asleep again.

The blackbird flew down to the empty bowl, and the mouse crept near. The hedgehog unrolled himself and put his snout over the edge.

'It's quite empty,' he said, with a sigh.

'Quite,' said the blackbird.

'All gone,' said the little mouse and a tear splashed on to his nose.

'How foolish we were to quarrel about it!' said the blackbird. 'There was enough and spare for all of us, if only we had been content to share it in peace. With our quarrelling we woke that horrid cat, and now there is no bread and milk left at all.'

'We will be good to one another in future,' said the hedgehog.

'Yes, let's,' said the mouse.

'And as for that horrid cat,' said the blackbird in a very loud voice, 'he will be punished one day!'

The cat woke up, and heard what the blackbird said. He leapt down and sprang towards the three round the bowl – but no one was there!

The blackbird was at the top of a tree, the mouse was in his hole and the hedgehog hurrying to his ditch.

'Silly things!' said the cat and washed himself all over again, to show everyone that he didn't care what was said about him.

Lucky we had been content to start it [illegible] with our quarrelling, [illegible] that [illegible] and still [illegible].

We will be good to one another in future, said the [illegible].

[illegible] said [illegible].

And a [illegible] and [illegible].

[illegible] when the [illegible] down and [illegible] towards the [illegible] and the [illegible].

The [illegible] was at the top of a tree. The [illegible] was [illegible] and [illegible].

[illegible] said the [illegible] and [illegible] himself all [illegible] to [illegible] at no [illegible] what [illegible].

Cosy's Good Turn

Cosy's Good Turn

BUNDLE CAME running into the garden to find Cosy. He had an old and rather smelly kipper in his mouth.

He dropped it and barked for Cosy. 'Cosy! Cosy! Now where can that cat be? What on earth's the good of finding this nice old kipper for her, out of Mrs Brown's dustbin, if she doesn't come when she's called?'

Cosy sat on top of the wall, washing her face with her paws. She had heard Bundle barking, but she didn't hurry down to see what he wanted.

I expect he wants to play chase-my-tail or roll-over-and-over, thought Cosy. *What silly games he knows!*

'Woof, woof!' barked Bundle, and then a faint

smell of kipper came to Cosy's nose. She sniffed. Then she leapt straight down from the wall and ran to Bundle, her tail up in the air behind her.

'I thought you were never coming,' said Bundle. 'I've done you a good turn, Cosy. I've found you an old kipper. It's been eaten a bit, but it smells fine. I was just going to eat it myself if you didn't come at once!'

Cosy purred, and rubbed herself against Bundle's silky coat. 'You're kind to do me a good turn,' she said.

'Well,' said Bundle, watching Cosy eat the kipper, 'you know what Mistress always says, don't you? She says, "One good turn deserves another."'

'Does she really?' said Cosy. 'Well, you do me another good turn then, Bundle. I don't mind.'

'Don't be silly. It doesn't mean that I do you another good turn,' said Bundle. 'It means that you do me one – in return for mine, you see.'

'Oh,' said Cosy, crunching up the last of the kipper. 'All right. I'll do you a good turn too. The very next thing you want, tell me and I'll get it for you.'

'Thanks very much,' said Bundle, pleased. 'I'll let you know when I want something. You do smell nice, Cosy. You smell of kipper now, not cat. Come and lie down beside me so that I can keep on sniffing you.'

Now, the very next day was hot, so hot that Bundle lay and panted with his tongue out. Someone had spilt his water and there was none to drink. There were no puddles anywhere. It was too far to go to the stream. But oh, how thirsty he was!

'You look silly with your tongue out like that,' said Cosy. 'Do put it back.'

'It comes out as soon as I put it in,' said Bundle. 'It always does that when I'm hot. Oh, how thirsty I am! Is there any milk about, Cosy? There's no water.'

'I've drunk all mine,' said Cosy. 'I'll go and see if there's any milk in the larder, Bundle. If there is, I know how to knock the jug over and spill the milk on the floor. Then you can come and lick it up.'

But the larder door was shut. It always was when

Cosy was anywhere about. She went back to Bundle and lay down.

'The larder door's shut,' she said. 'You'll just have to be thirsty, Bundle.'

'Well, why can't you do me that good turn you promised me?' said Bundle. 'I'm very thirsty, and you ought to do something about it. You do me my good turn now. Get me some milk to drink!'

'If I knew where the milk came from I'd go and get some for you,' said Cosy. 'Where does the milkman get his milk from?'

'From a cow, silly,' said Bundle. 'All our milk comes from cows.'

'Does it really?' said Cosy in surprise. 'Well, I never knew that before! How kind of the cows! I know, Bundle – I'll take a jug and go and ask that big red-and-white cow in the field for some milk for you. That would be an awfully good turn, wouldn't it?'

'Yes,' said Bundle, panting. 'Hurry up then!'

Cosy got a little jug. Then she set off to the fields. Daisy, the big red-and-white cow, was lying down in a cool corner, chewing.

Cows are always chewing, they never seem to stop, thought Cosy. 'Hallo, Daisy! Do you think I could possibly have some milk, please?' she asked.

'Well,' said Daisy, still chewing, 'one good turn deserves another, you know. There's some lovely dark green grass in the next field, all long and juicy, but I can't reach it over the hedge myself. You go and get me a bit of that and I'll fill your jug for you.'

'All right,' said Cosy, and she ran to the hedge. She squeezed through it and looked about for the grass. She soon saw it growing by a moist ditch, long and juicy. Clopper the horse was standing near it, munching.

Cosy ran to get the grass. She began pulling it up. Clopper stopped munching and stared straight at her.

'Hey!' he said. 'That's my grass. It's the best grass in the whole field.'

'Oh,' said Cosy. 'Well, I want some for Daisy the cow, then she'll give me some milk. Can't I take some?'

'Now look here, one good turn deserves another,' said Clopper. 'You can have some of my grass if you'll do something for me.'

'I seem to be doing no end of good turns,' said Cosy.

'Well, I'm longing for a nice green apple,' said Clopper. 'See that cottage over there? Well, in the back garden there's an apple tree, and it's got fine green apples on it. You get me one of those and I'll let you take some of that grass.'

'All right,' said Cosy, and she ran over the field towards the cottage. She jumped up on the wall around it and then down into the garden. Then in a second she was up the apple tree.

She bumped her head hard against the biggest green apple she could see. It fell to the ground with a bump. Cosy was just about to run down the tree when she heard a cross voice.

'What are you doing up there, cat, knocking down my apples?'

Down below was a plump woman, trying to mend a clothes line so that she could hang out her washing. She was looking up at Cosy, surprised and cross.

'Well, you see, I wanted to get an apple for Clopper,' said Cosy. 'Could I have the one I knocked down?'

'Well, one good turn deserves another,' said the woman. 'If you'll go and borrow Mrs Miggle's rope for me, then I'll give you the apple. My clothes line is broken and I must have another!'

'Another good turn!' sighed Cosy, and ran down the lane to the next cottage, where Mrs Miggle was sitting in the sun, shelling peas.

'May I borrow your rope, please?' asked Cosy. 'You see, if I take it to your next-door neighbour, she will give me an apple for Clopper, and he will give me his best grass for Daisy, and she will give me milk for Bundle. I am trying to do him a good turn.'

'So you want my rope!' said Mrs Miggle. 'Well,

what I always say is, "One good turn deserves another." If I lend you my rope, you must do something for me. You run down to the old man who lives at the corner, and ask him to let me have just a few more peas. I haven't enough. Take this basket with you.'

'I keep on and on doing good turns!' said Cosy, but she ran off with the basket in her mouth. She soon came to the cottage at the corner. The old man was indoors, looking into his larder. He seemed rather cross.

'Please,' said Cosy, 'may I have a few peas? Mrs Miggle hasn't enough.'

'I'll go and pick them,' said the old man. 'I like to do people a good turn. But one good turn deserves another, you know, little cat. You can do me a good turn, while I pick the peas.'

'I thought you were going to say that,' said poor Cosy.

'Now just have a look in this larder of mine!' said the old man. 'Mice have been in it again. One ran away just as I opened the door. You catch me those mice by the time I come back and I'll give you the peas!'

He went out and Cosy sat down quietly behind the door. She could smell plenty of mice, no doubt about that.

Well, anyway, at least I shall be doing myself a good turn now, as well as the old man, she thought, *because I rather like catching mice!*

Soon Cosy had caught three mice. The old man came with the basket half full of peas. He was delighted to see what Cosy had done for him.

'You've done me a good turn,' he said. 'And you've done my cat a good turn too – she's too old to catch mice now. Here are the peas. Remember what I said? "One good turn deserves another!"'

'Goodbye!' said Cosy, and she left the cottage, taking the peas with her.

She went to Mrs Miggle's and put the basket down. 'Here are the peas,' she said. 'Now may I borrow the rope?'

'Here it is,' said Mrs Miggle, and gave it to her. 'Thank you. You see what I meant when I said, "One good turn–"'

But Cosy didn't even stop to listen. She tore off to the woman next door, trailing the rope out behind her like a long snake.

'Well, I thought you were never coming!' said the little woman quite crossly. 'I've been waiting such a time. Now, take your apple and go. And always remember, "One good–"'

'I know it by heart, thank you,' said Cosy quite rudely, and then she ran off with the apple. She came to Clopper and rolled it at his feet.

'What a time you've been,' said Clopper. 'I had quite given you up. I suppose you've been chattering away to someone. Take what grass you want – and remember, "One–"'

'I don't want to remember it,' said Cosy crossly, dragging up the grass. 'I've been doing nothing but good turns for ages and ages. You may have done me one good turn, but I tell you I've done heaps! I can't seem to stop doing them. I–'

'What a lot you've got to say,' said Clopper. 'Ah – now you've got your mouth full of grass and you won't be able to talk. Good. Now remember, "One–"'

But Cosy had fled through the hedge and was on her way to the shady corner in the field where Daisy the cow still lay, chewing away. The little empty jug lay beside her.

'Here's your grass,' said Cosy, and dropped it right down beside Daisy.

'I don't really know if I want it now,' said Daisy. 'You've been so long.'

'Well!' said Cosy crossly. 'Of all the ungrateful, unkind–'

'All right, all right,' said the cow hurriedly. 'I'll have it. Don't lose your temper. You should always do a good turn cheerfully and quickly.'

'Don't talk to me about good turns,' said Cosy.

'Just you do yours, Daisy, and give me some milk for poor old thirsty Bundle. I've been so busy doing good turns for everybody!'

Daisy filled the jug with creamy milk, which looked simply lovely. 'Now don't spill it,' she said. 'And remember–'

But Cosy wasn't going to remember anything but the milk. Thank goodness she had got it at last! She went carefully across the field, through the hedge and into the garden. She looked about for Bundle. Ah, there he was, in the corner where it was cool. How pleased he would be to see the milk! Cosy trotted over and put the jug down carefully beside him.

'There you are, Bundle!' she said. 'Lovely milk for you.'

Bundle looked down his nose at it. 'What, milk again?' he said. 'I don't want any more. Mistress came out some time ago and filled your dish with rice pudding and milk. I ate it all up, and I can tell you the milk was very good! But I'm full up now and I don't want any more. It really makes me feel sick to look at all that milk.'

'Well!' cried poor Cosy in a rage, and lost her temper altogether. She picked up the jug and threw it at Bundle. The milk spilt and went all over his silky coat. He was very angry.

'You horrid little cat! Now look what you've done! There's milk all over my coat. And I thought you wanted to do me a good turn, not a bad one!'

'Well, I've tried,' said Cosy and tears trickled down her nose. 'I've done ever so many good turns. I'm hot and tired and thirsty. I've been ever so far and got ever so many things for people. And when I come back with my good turn for you, Bundle, you don't want it. I feel very upset. And the milk's upset too, and I do so badly want a drink! You've had all my dinner too. Why did I ever try to do you a good turn? It's all wasted!'

'You can always do me another one some other time,' said Bundle. But that wasn't the right thing to say at all.

'What! Another good turn!' cried Cosy. 'No, no, Bundle – you can do all the good turns in future. Do you know, I went to Daisy for some milk, and she sent me to Clopper for some special grass she wanted, and Clopper sent me to an apple tree for an apple, and the woman there sent me to Mrs Miggle's for a rope, and–'

'Goodness gracious!' said Bundle.

'–and Mrs Miggle sent me to the old man at the corner for some more peas, and he told me to catch his mice!' wept poor Cosy. 'And then I had to go back and take the peas to Mrs Miggle, and take the rope to the apple woman, and take the apple to Clopper, and take the grass to Daisy, and bring the milk to you, and–'

'And I'd had some, and you upset the milk in a temper,' said Bundle. 'Poor Cosy! What a shame! But now I'll do you a good turn, if you like! I'll sit quite still and let you lick all the milk that is dripping off my coat. Think what a nice meal that will be for you.'

So Cosy sat and licked all the milk off Bundle's

coat, and got a lot of hairs down her throat. Now she is still on the wall again, washing herself – and do you know what she is thinking?

'I wonder whether that was really a good turn that Bundle did me, letting me lick the milk off his coat?' she is saying to herself. 'Or have I done *him* a good turn again? I've cleaned his coat for him, haven't I, and saved him from having a bath! Now, who did the good turn then?'

What do you think?

The Rabbit's Whiskers

The Rabbit's Whiskers

MR WOFFLES was a large toy rabbit, and he lived in a nice little house in Toyland. He had fine whiskers, and he was very, very proud of them.

Now, one day he went to the hairdresser and asked for a haircut. The hairs on his ears were really getting rather long, and as he wanted to go to a party at the teddy bear's that evening he wanted to look smart.

The hairdresser was a wooden doll with black hair painted on his head so that it looked very neat and smooth. He took up his scissors and began to snip.

Snip, snap, snip, snap! went his scissors. Some of

the hairs went into Mr Woffle's eyes, and he shut them tight. When he opened them again, oh my goodness, what a shock he got!

The hairdresser had cut off all his fine whiskers!

'Ooh!' shouted Mr Woffles in dismay. 'I say! Why did you cut off my whiskers? Just look at that! Oh my, I do look a fright.'

'Sorry, sir, but you didn't say I wasn't to,' said the hairdresser.

'I didn't say you were to either!' groaned the poor rabbit. 'Now what am I to do? No rabbit goes out without whiskers, not even a toy rabbit like me. And I'm to go to a party tonight!'

He went groaning out of the hairdresser's and quite forgot to pay his bill. The hairdresser didn't like to remind him because he felt very sorry to have made such a dreadful mistake about the whiskers.

Mr Woffles felt so bad that he turned quite pale, and when he met his friends, Mrs Plush Duck and Mr Sailor Doll, they wondered what was the matter.

'Don't you feel well?' they asked. 'And oh – what's happened to your fine whiskers?'

Then Mr Woffles told them, and they were just as upset as he was.

'Never mind,' said Mrs Plush Duck, thinking hard. 'Come with me to the gooseberry bed. Gooseberries grow whiskers, you know, and maybe we can get some from them for you.'

So they all went to the gooseberry bushes and had a look at the gooseberries.

'Well, they certainly grow whiskers,' said Mr Woffles the rabbit, looking at the hairy gooseberries. 'But they are such little ones. They wouldn't be any use to me.'

'No, they wouldn't,' agreed Mr Sailor Doll. 'Well, let's think of something else.'

So they thought and thought, and then Mr Sailor Doll remembered that he had seen a lot of whiskery-looking things lying in the pine wood not very far away.

'The pine trees drop them,' he said. 'They are long and brown, and might do quite well for you, Mr Woffles.'

'Oh, do you mean the pine needles?' asked Mrs Plush Duck. 'Yes, they might do. Let's go and see.'

'I don't think I should very much like to wear pine needles,' said Mr Woffles. 'They sound rather sharp to me.'

'Just come and see them,' said his friends. 'They lie about under the trees in hundreds.'

So they went to the pine woods, and picked up a great many pine needles. They stuck them into Mr Woffles's cheeks, and he didn't like them at all. 'No,' he said firmly. 'They won't do. They're too stiff, and they hurt me, and they look silly. We must think of something else.'

So they threw them away, and tried hard to think of another idea. They were sitting there thinking when who should come along but Waggy, the lovely spaniel dog that lived just outside Toyland.

He was very friendly with Old Mother Hubbard who lived not far away, and often used to come to see her.

'What's the matter?' he asked the three toys, seeing them sitting so sadly together.

'The hairdresser cut off my whiskers this morning,' said Mr Woffles. 'We are trying to think of where I can get some new ones to wear at the teddy bear's party tonight. We've looked at the gooseberry whiskers, but they're too small. And we've tried these pine needles whiskers and they're too sharp and stiff.'

Waggy sat down and scratched his silky head. 'Let me see–' he said, and just then Mrs Plush Duck cried out in excitement. 'Look!' she said. 'You've scratched out a lot of lovely long silky hairs from your head! Mr Woffles, surely those would make fine whiskers for you!'

Mr Woffles picked up the hairs that had fallen from Waggy's coat and tried them against his cheeks.

'How do they look?' he asked.

'Fine!' said everyone. 'They show up well against your sandy cheeks.'

'Let's go to the Toy Hospital and get them stuck on for you,' said Mrs Plush Duck. So Waggy, Mr Woffles, Mr Sailor Doll and Mrs Plush Duck all went to the Toy Hospital, where broken dolls were mended, wheels put on carts and stitches put into toy animals whose sawdust was leaking out.

The toy doctor took a brush full of glue and dotted little specks of it over Mr Woffles's cheeks. Then he lightly stuck the black hairs into the dots of glue.

'They will be dried hard in ten minutes,' he said. 'Then they will be quite all right.'

And in ten minutes, sure enough, the dots of glue were hard, and dear me, Mr Woffles' new whiskers looked very grand indeed. They stuck out from his cheeks and were much longer than the ones he had had before.

'I'm much obliged to you for letting me have your long hairs,' he said to Waggy.

'Oh, I'm very pleased about it,' said Waggy. 'You do look fine! Everyone at the party will wonder where you got such fine whiskers from!'

And so they did – even the stuffed tiger, whose whiskers were longer than any other toy's, kept looking and looking at Mr Woffles. He had a lovely time, and when he saw that the wooden hairdresser hadn't anyone to dance with, he forgave him for cutting off his whiskers and went to ask him if he would like a dance.

That was really very nice of him, wasn't it?

Who-Who-Who-Who?

Who-Who-Who-Who?

OLD MOTHER Twinkle kept six fine brown hens. She was a poor old woman, and she was very glad to have the nice big eggs from her hens.

She ate some and some she sold. Although she was poor she gave away a few too.

'What I should do without my dear old hens I don't know!' she said. 'They give me breakfast, dinner and tea, and they bring me in money to buy myself bread and sugar and tea.'

Old Mother Twinkle knew all the birds and animals around. She fed the red robin in winter, and put out a bone for the tits to swing on. She liked the little prickly hedgehog that sometimes came into her garden, and she gave him a bowl of bread and milk to eat.

She kept titbits for all the dogs and cats that visited her, and if ever an animal or bird was in trouble she would help it.

She put young birds back into their nests when they fell out. She took a young rabbit from a trap in the woods, and nursed it until its poor hurt paw was better. She helped a robin with a broken leg, and fed him till he could hop again.

One day she heard a hissing noise in a tree, and she peeped inside to see what made it.

A little brown owl was there, all alone. The old woman was surprised.

'Why are you here?' she asked. 'There is no one here with you. Your brothers and sisters are gone, baby owl. Your mother and father are gone too. Why did you not go with them? You are old enough to fly.'

The owl made a funny snoring noise. 'One of my feet is caught, and I cannot get it free. I could not follow my family. They left me here alone, and I am half starved!'

'Poor little creature!' said Mother Twinkle. 'I will help you to get out. Don't drive your sharp claws into me, or you will hurt me. Let me put my hand down and set your foot free.'

The owl understood that she wanted to help him, and he lay quite still. He did not strike at her with his sharp, curved beak, or with his one free foot, with its strong claws.

The old lady set him free. He climbed up to the edge of the hole and looked out. He was weak because he had had no food for two or three days.

'Come with me,' said the old woman. 'Step on to my shoulder, owl, and I will take you home. I will feed you and nurse you till you are strong enough to fly, and hunt for yourself.'

The owl stepped on to her shoulder. He held on to

her dress with his curving claws, but he did not touch her soft skin. He was very glad and grateful.

He stayed with Mother Twinkle for a few days, and she fed him well. He was soon quite all right again, and wanted to go and find his family.

'I must leave you,' he said. 'I must go and join my brothers and sisters, and learn to catch beetles, and mice and all kinds of other food. I will come back and tell you how I get on.'

He flew away at night, very softly, on his big brown wings. His great big eyes could see very clearly in the darkness. Mother Twinkle missed him when he went.

But he was back again early the next morning. 'I had a lovely time,' he said. 'I caught sixteen beetles, and I even managed to catch a mouse.'

'How did you catch it?' asked the old woman. 'Did you peck it?'

'Oh no,' said the owl. 'I was flying quietly over a field – like this – looking downwards, and my big eyes caught sight of something moving. I felt sure it was a mouse. So I pounced down at once, feet first – like this.'

'Why did you pounce with your feet first?' asked the old woman.

'Look at my feet,' said the owl and he held out a foot for the old woman to see. 'Do you see those strong curved claws? Well, when they catch hold of a mouse or rat, they meet, and make a kind of trap. No animal can get out of it!'

'I see,' said the old woman. 'Yes, brown owl, you have strange feet. The eagle has feet like you too. But wouldn't a mouse or rat try to bite your legs? You might get a very nasty bite.'

'I know,' said the owl. 'But look at my legs, Dame Twinkle. Do you see how thickly they are feathered – right down to the toes? A rat or mouse would only get a mouthful of feathers if it tried to bite me – it could not get through all these soft feathers to my leg.'

'That is a very good idea,' said the old woman.

'Now, owl, hadn't you better sit quietly in a corner? You had a lot to eat last night, you know. I don't know how you manage all those hard beetle shells, and the skin and bones of a mouse. You really must sit quietly after such a meal!'

'You needn't worry about that,' said the owl. 'Although I swallow the beetles and mice whole, I spit out their shells and skins and bones afterwards.'

'Well, really!' said Mother Twinkle. 'If you are going to do that, brown owl, I think you had better sit in the shed, not in my kitchen.'

So the brown owl went and sat all day in the shed. He spat up the shells of the beetles, and the skin and bones of the mouse. It was not a rude thing to do, because all owls do that. Mother Twinkle popped her head in the shed once or twice, and he watched her through slits in his eyelids, half asleep. When she went to the back of the shed for something, he turned his head right round on his neck to watch her. It was extraordinary to see.

'Goodness! It looks as if you can put your head back to front!' said Mother Twinkle. 'Now I'm going to collect my hens' eggs, brown owl. I shan't disturb you any more.'

But she did disturb him, for she came in crying. 'Someone has stolen my eggs,' she said. 'Oh, how unkind! Someone has stolen my eggs!'

The owl opened his eyes wide. 'Who?' he asked.

'I don't know,' wept the poor old woman. 'If my eggs are stolen like this, I shall have no breakfast and no dinner and no tea. Who can it be?'

'I will find out tonight,' said the owl. So that night, when it was dark, the owl swept softly out of the shed on his silent wings, and went to find his family again. He told them about the old woman's stolen eggs. 'Who stole them, I wonder?' he said.

'Who-Who-Who-Who!' hooted the two biggest owls. 'We'll find out! Who-Who-Who-Who!'

And that night, over the countryside, the old woman heard the owls looking for the robber who took her eggs.

'Who-Who-Who-Who!' they cried. 'Who-Who-Who-Who!'

'Listen to the owls hooting!' said everyone.

It was the rat who had stolen the eggs. He had been to the hen run that night, and had taken another egg. He had eaten it, and was just going back home, when he heard the owls hooting above him. He crouched down at once, close to the grass.

The father owl saw him crouch. 'Who-Who-Who-Who!' he hooted, and pounced downwards. His strong claws caught hold of the fierce rat. The rat squealed.

'Here is the robber!' cried the owl to his family. 'Come and see! He has egg-yellow on his nose!'

'Let me go!' squealed the bad rat, and he tried to snap at the owl's legs with his sharp teeth. But the legs were thickly feathered, and the rat only got feathers in his mouth. He snapped again. It was no use. He could not bite the owl.

'You won't steal eggs from old Mother Twinkle

any more!' said the little brown owl, as the big owl flew up into the air with the rat. That was the end of him. The little brown owl flew back to Mother Twinkle to tell her, the very next day.

'The rat was the robber,' he said, settling down in the shed. 'It's a good thing we owls eat rats and mice, and not just seeds and fruits, Mother Twinkle, or we could not have caught and eaten your robber for you!'

'Do you know who is a very, very good friend to me?' said Mother Twinkle, stroking the owl's soft feathers.

'Who-Who-Who-Who?' asked the owl sleepily.

'You-You-You-You!' said Mother Twinkle. And that made them both laugh!

a more [illegible] little brown owl as the big owl flew up into the tree with [illegible]. That was the end of [illegible] on [illegible] to Uncle Twink [illegible] the very next day.

The [illegible] and [illegible] down in [illegible] good thing [illegible] and not [illegible] Twinkle [illegible] we could not have [illegible] and [illegible]

[illegible] you know [illegible] good friend [illegible] said Mother Twinkle [illegible] [illegible]

"Who-Who-Who!" [illegible]

"[illegible]" said Mother Twinkle [illegible] [illegible]

He Was Clever After All!

He Was Clever After All!

THE LITTLE dog next door was always coming through the hedge into Robin's garden. He was black and brown, and he had a short, waggy tail and very nice brown eyes.

'I shall teach you tricks,' said Robin to Wagger the dog. 'There's a boy at school who has a marvellous dog. He can sit up and beg. He can shut the door. And he can even roll over and lie still on the ground.'

Wagger wagged his tail. He liked little boys very much. They nearly always had a ball, and Wagger loved a ball. He would run for miles, round and round and up and down, if he had a ball to chase.

But Wagger wasn't much good at learning tricks. He couldn't seem to sit up on his hind legs at all. He fell over at once.

'Wagger! Don't be so silly!' said Robin. 'Other dogs can sit up. Why can't you? Look, I'll hold you up for a bit, then I'll gently let go, and you'll find yourself sitting up beautifully. Just keep a nice straight back. Now, sit up! Beg!'

But Wagger fell over as soon as Robin took away his hand. It wasn't a bit of good.

'You're a silly dog,' said Robin in disgust. 'Mother, Wagger hasn't any brains at all.'

'He's too old to learn tricks,' said Mother. 'Dogs should learn when they are puppies, not when they are five years old, like Wagger.'

Wagger looked longingly at the ball on the garden chair. What about a game, his brown eyes said, and he barked. 'Wuff! What about a ball game?'

'No. No game for you, because you haven't learnt a single trick,' said Robin crossly. 'And no biscuit either.

Go back home. I don't want to play with a silly dog like you.'

So Wagger went sadly back through the hedge. But he came to Robin the next day, still hoping to run after the ball.

'I'll just see if you are a bit cleverer today,' said Robin, and he tried once more to teach Wagger a trick. But no, Wagger couldn't learn. He just didn't seem to understand at all. Robin got really very cross.

'You're not even trying! You must be the silliest dog in the world. I won't play with you, or let you come into my garden any more! I'll block up the hole in the hedge.'

So he did, and poor Wagger couldn't get through any more and whined sadly. Why was that boy so cross with him? Wagger didn't understand.

Now, that afternoon Robin went to tea all by himself with his granny. She lived quite a long way off, but Robin knew the way very well. He set off, and soon got there. He was pleased to see the lovely tea that Granny had got for him.

But, oh, dear, when he set out to go home after tea, there was a thick fog everywhere! Robin went down the street and turned the corner. But after a bit, he stopped. Everywhere looked so different in the fog. He couldn't see the houses and shops he knew so well. If he wasn't careful he would be lost!

And very soon he *was* lost. He wandered about street after street, not meeting anyone, wondering where he was. Should he go to one of the houses and ask where he was? Would they think he was very silly? Oh, dear, what a dreadful fog this was!

Suddenly he heard a patter of feet and a little whine behind him. Then a bark. Wuff! Then a wet tongue touched his hand. Robin bent down and ran his hand over the little dog beside his knee.

'Wagger! Is it you?' he said, and Wagger barked joyfully. 'Wuff, wuff! Yes, it's me!'

'Are you lost too? Poor Wagger!' said Robin. 'I'm quite, quite lost. I wish I could take you home, but I can't. I don't know the way. Wait a bit, Wagger. Don't leave me. I'd rather be lost with you than lost all by myself. I've got a bit of string. I'll slip it under your collar and you can keep close beside me. You may be the silliest dog in the world but you're company, anyway!'

Robin slipped the string under Wagger's collar. There, now he couldn't run off and leave him.

Wagger began to pull at the string, and Robin had to follow him. 'Don't get us more lost, Wagger,' begged Robin. 'I'd better ask our way at one of these houses, I think.'

But Wagger wouldn't stop. He went on and on, turning corners and crossing roads, and he pulled Robin along behind him.

'Stop, Wagger!' cried Robin. 'We'll be in the next town soon, silly dog!'

Wagger suddenly stopped and pawed at a shut gate. And at the very same moment the door of the house opened, and somebody anxiously looked out.

Robin saw who it was at once. His mother!

'Mother!' he shouted. 'Oh, Mother! I was lost. I didn't know I was home, outside my own house. Oh, Mother, isn't Wagger clever, he's brought me all the way home by himself.'

Wagger went indoors with Robin, wagging his tail. He didn't think he had done anything clever at all. A dog didn't need his eyes to see his way home, his nose would tell him! He had gone for a walk by himself and suddenly smelt Robin. Poor Robin, he had seemed upset, and Wagger had been glad to lead him safely home.

'Mother, I was wrong about Wagger. He isn't silly at all. He's very, very clever,' said Robin. 'And he's nice too. I was horrid and cross to him. I even blocked up the hedge to stop him coming through, but when he found me, all lost by myself, he took me safely home. Mother, may I give him some biscuits?'

So, much to his surprise, Wagger had a wonderful feast of biscuits and was made a great fuss of, which pleased his loving, doggy heart very much. And the next day, what joy! Robin unblocked the hedge and called Wagger loudly.

'Wagger! Come and have a game of ball! Come on! No tricks, old fellow, but *ball*!'

And now Wagger plays ball each day with Robin, and you should see the clever way he chases it and catches it in his mouth.

'You may be silly at some things,' Robin says to him, 'but you're very, very clever at others!'

The Three Pixies and the Cats

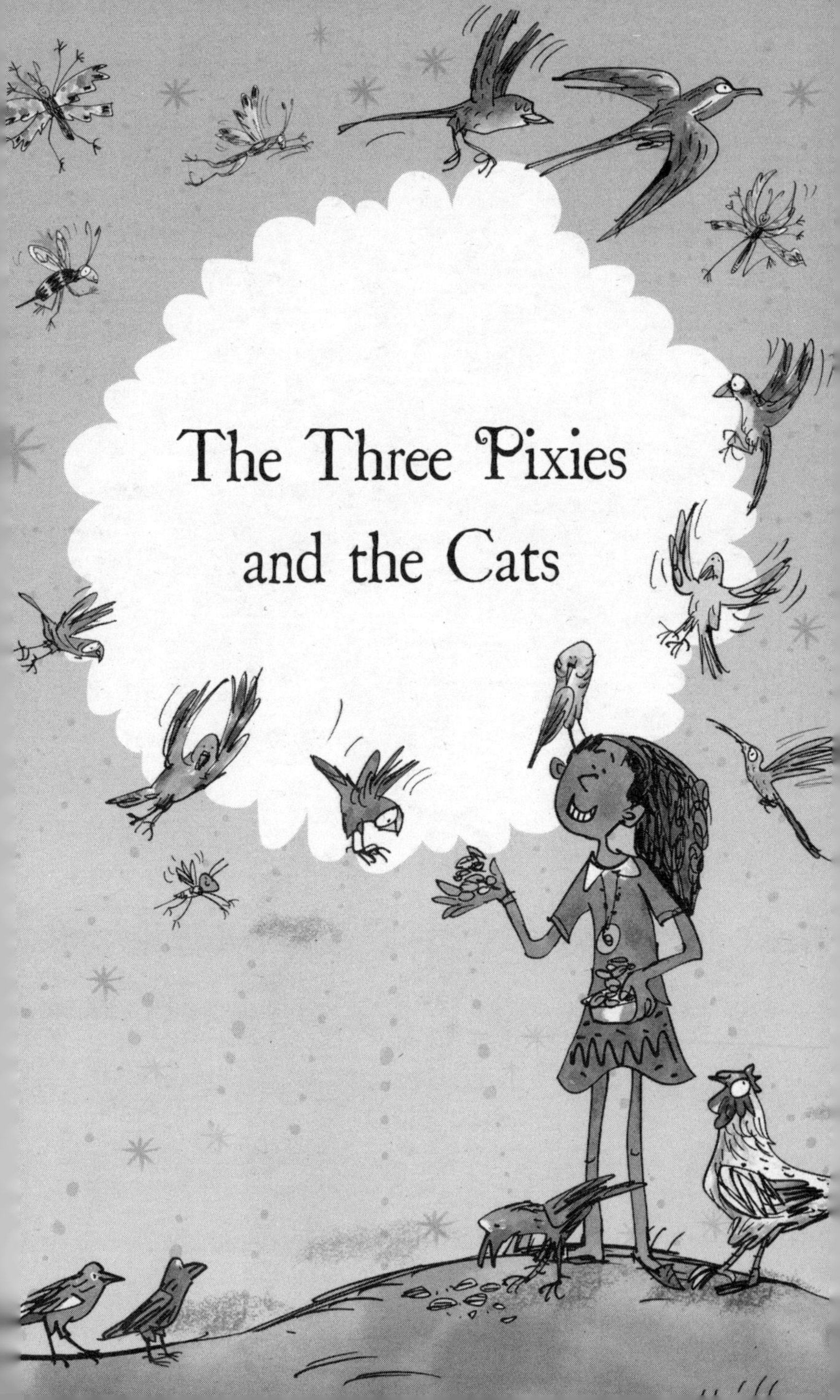

The Three Pixies and the Cats

PERI, PATTER and Pipkin were getting their dinner ready one day when Peri found that someone had been nibbling at the cheese.

'Hallo!' he said, lifting up the dish. 'Which of you two has been nibbling our cheese?'

'*I* haven't,' said Patter, looking quite offended.

'And I wouldn't *dream* of doing such a thing!' said Pipkin.

'Well, then, it must be mice,' said Peri, and he looked solemnly at the others. 'Mice in the larder! This will never do, will it? We shan't have a thing left. Our bacon will go. Our cheese will be nibbled.

Our bread will be eaten. We simply *must* get rid of those mice.'

'There's only one way,' said Patter.

'What's that?' asked the other two.

'Get a cat!' said Patter. 'That's what we must do.'

'Right!' said Peri. 'We'll look out for a good mouser. We'll let her sleep in the larder at night and then the mice will soon go.'

'And so will the milk and the bacon and the fish!' said Pipkin. 'No – we'll keep her in the kitchen. The mice will smell her out in the kitchen, and they'll scurry off. If they come into the kitchen she'll catch them.'

Now, that afternoon Peri went out to buy some chocolate. At the shop was a beautiful black cat with green eyes. She lay on the counter and blinked lazily at Peri.

He remembered the mice in the larder. 'I say,' he said, 'is that cat a good mouser?'

'Splendid,' said the shopkeeper.

'Will you sell her to me?' asked Peri.

'No,' said the man. 'We're fond of her. But she's got some black kittens exactly like herself. You can have one of those for nothing, if you like, if you promise to give her a good home. We want to find homes for them now.'

'Oh, thanks very much,' said Peri pleased. The man went into his room at the back, and came out with a basketful of fine black kittens. There were three of them, all with green eyes like their mother. Peri picked up one of them and it cuddled against him.

'I'll have this one,' he said. 'It's a darling. Thank you very much.'

Peri went off with the kitten. He had to go to fetch his boots from the mender's, so he took the kitten with him. It was quite a long walk but the kitten didn't mind. It loved Peri.

Now, not long after Peri had gone out, Patter yawned and stood up. 'I'm going to get a paper,' he said. 'Then I'll go along and see Josie, Click and

Bun in the treehouse. Shan't be very long, Pipkin.'

He went off down the street to the shop. It was the samc shop that sold chocolate to Peri. Patter walked in and grinned at the shopkeeper.

'A *Pixie Times*, please,' he said.

'Here you are,' said the man. 'How's the kitten?'

Patter stared at him in surprise. 'What did you say?' he asked.

'I said, "How's the kitten?"' said the man.

'What kitten?' asked Patter.

'The kitten you took away,' said the man.

'I didn't take any kitten away,' said Patter.

'You did!' said the man. 'You took it away under your coat.'

'You're making a mistake,' said Patter, 'I have no use for a kitten!' And then he suddenly remembered the mice in the larder, and he looked at the shopkeeper. 'Oh, I *could* do with a kitten!' he said. 'Have you got one to spare?'

'What do you want another one for?' asked the man.

'I don't want another one,' said Patter. 'I haven't got one at all. But I do want one.'

'Well, it's a bit funny, all this,' said the man doubtfully. He went into his back room and brought out the basket with two black kittens in. 'If you are really sure you didn't take one of my kittens just now, you can have one of these.'

'Oh, thanks very much,' said Patter, pleased, and he picked up the nearest kitten. It was such a little dear, and cuddled up to Patter at once.

Patter went off with it, thinking how glad the others would be to see the dear little kitten he had got. He set off to the treehouse to visit Josie, Click and Bun, to show them the kitten.

Now Pipkin was bored at being left all alone in the house. He thought he would go and buy some sweets. So up he got and down the street he went. He came to the shop that sold chocolate, papers and sweets, and went inside.

'Some fruit drops, please,' he said.

'These?' asked the shopkeeper, and gave him a packet. Then he looked closely at Pipkin. 'How's the kitten getting on?' he asked.

'Don't be silly,' said Pipkin. 'I haven't got a kitten – or a puppy, or a duckling or a lion cub either!'

'That's not funny,' said the shopkeeper, offended. 'You took one of my kittens just now. I just wanted to know how the little thing was getting on.'

'Well, how do I know what a kitten that I haven't got is doing?' said Pipkin. 'What do you suppose it is doing? Drinking water from the goldfish bowl, or catching mice in my larder?'

Now, as soon as Pipkin had said that, it reminded him of the real mice in his larder, and he stared eagerly at the shopkeeper. 'I say – I would *like* a kitten very much,' he said. 'I suppose you haven't one to spare?'

'Look here,' said the man, 'am I going to spend all afternoon giving you my kittens – and then have you come back and say that you haven't got them?'

'Don't be silly,' said Pipkin. 'Do you suppose I'd ask you for a kitten if I'd got dozens?'

'Well, no, I suppose you wouldn't,' said the shopkeeper. 'But what do you *do* with them? You walk out of the shop with a kitten under your coat – and then you come back and say you don't know anything about them. It's all very mysterious to me.'

'And to me too,' said Pipkin. 'But all the same, if you've got a kitten, I'd love to have it.'

'Well, it's the last one I've got,' said the shopkeeper, going into his back room. 'And don't you dare to come back and ask for another.'

He brought the last little black kitten out, and gave it to Pipkin. 'Thanks very much,' said Pipkin, pleased, for the little thing was a real pet, and snuggled up to him most lovingly. He went out of the shop with it. He thought he would go straight home and pop the kitten into the warm kitchen and wait for the others to come home so that they might have a surprise.

He opened the kitchen door and put the kitten there. Then he went upstairs to wash. As soon as he had gone upstairs, Patter came home with his kitten. He popped it into the kitchen too, and shut the door so that it couldn't get out. Then he went to hang his things up in the hall. As he was doing that, Peri came home.

Peri brushed past him and went to the kitchen. He popped his kitten in too, thinking that it would be a marvellous surprise for the others when they went into the kitchen for tea.

'Patter! Pipkin! Come along and see the surprise I've got for you!' cried Peri. The others hurried to him and they all went to the kitchen.

They opened the door – and there in the middle of the floor were three black kittens all playing happily together.

Now, this was a great shock to all the pixies, for they each knew they had only put *one* kitten into the kitchen – and in some extraordinary way that one kitten seemed to have turned into three! All the pixies stared in amazement.

Then they rubbed their eyes and looked once again at the three black kittens, all exactly alike, with their little tails and bright green eyes.

'My eyes have gone wrong,' said Peri. 'I'm seeing three instead of one.'

'So am I,' said Patter.

'And I am too,' said Pipkin. 'This is dreadful. We shall have to wear glasses. To think that my kitten has changed into three!'

'*My* kitten, you mean!' said Patter in surprise.

'No, *mine*!' said Peri in amazement. 'I brought the kitten home – and I can't imagine why it's turned into three.'

The kittens ran to the pixies. One went to Peri, one to Pipkin and one to Patter. The pixies stared at each other. 'There must be *three* kittens really, after all!' said Peri. 'But where did they all come from?'

'I got one from the shopkeeper,' said Patter.

'And I got one from him too,' said Pipkin.

'Well, so did I,' said Peri. 'The man must have been most surprised!'

'He was!' said Patter and Pipkin. 'Gracious – what are we to do now? Shall we take two kittens back?'

'No – the man will think we are *very* silly if we go back again and take the kittens with us!' said Peri. 'We'll have to keep them all!'

So they did – and if ever you visit the three pixies, you are sure to see three big black cats with green eyes sitting on the sofa – and you'll know how it is that there are three of them.

And, of course, there are *no* mice in the larder now!

The Tale of Cluck and Clopper

The Tale of Cluck and Clopper

'THERE'S THAT dog again!' said Cluck the hen, and ran away at top speed. All the other hens scuttled away too. Sam the dog was a tease. He loved chasing the hens and seeing them scamper off in fright.

He chased them now, first into one corner of the farmyard and then into another. What a time he had, barking and prancing!

One little hen squeezed through a gap in the hedge, and went into the field where the horses were kept. She found herself near a big horse who looked at the clucking hen in surprise.

'What's the matter?' said the horse.

'It's that dog,' said the hen. 'Can't you hear him chasing all the hens? We get so frightened.'

'Well, stay by me,' said the horse. 'What's your name? Mine is Clopper.'

'Mine is Cluck,' said the hen. 'I think I'm all right here. I'll just take a walk around this field and see if I can scratch up something to eat.'

So she set off by herself, looking into all the corners – and then, quite suddenly, she saw Sam the dog squeezing through the hedge near her. He had seen her through the leaves. Aha! Another hen to chase!

Cluck scampered away, clucking loudly. Sam pinned her into a corner, with a bush behind her. 'Cluck, cluck – cluck, cackle, cackle, CLUCK!' she cried. 'Help, help!'

Clopper the horse looked up and saw what was happening. He cantered over at once and neighed loudly. Then he said '*HROOOOOOMPH*' just like that, and Sam stopped prancing about and looked astonished.

'Off with you!' said Clopper, stamping his hoof. 'I said OFF WITH YOU! *HROOOOOOMPH!*'

Sam fled for his life, yelping. What an enormous animal a horse was when it stood right over you! He didn't like it at all.

'Thank you, Clopper. Thank you very much,' said Cluck gratefully. 'One of these days perhaps, I can do *you* a good turn – and help you.'

Clopper gave a loud neighing laugh. 'What! A little thing like you help a great big thing like me! Nonsense! You're not so important as all that, little hen – you could never be of any use to me.'

'Well – one good turn deserves another,' said Cluck. 'I would dearly *like* to help you, Clopper.'

She went off back to the farm – but often after that she came into the horse's field to see her big friend, and pecked happily between his feet.

Clopper didn't mind. The little hen amused him. She asked him all kinds of questions.

'Why do you have such big feet with no claws

or toes? Why do you wear a mane of hair? And dear me, Clopper, why is your tail cut so short? All the other horses have long tails that swish to and fro.'

'Mine's docked,' said Clopper. 'That means that it's been cut very short to make me look smart. I'm the only horse here with a docked tail. Don't you think I look smart?'

'Yes,' said Cluck, who thought Clopper was the smartest, cleverest, kindest horse in the world. 'It does seem silly to wear a long tail when you can have it cut short and look so neat.'

But, when the hot summer days came, Cluck changed her mind about tails. There were flies everywhere that month. Oh what a nuisance they were to the horses and the cows! They flew down to them in clouds, and walked about all over the big creatures, and often bit them.

The cows swung their long tails to and fro and beat them off. The horses swished their hairy tails, flicking off dozens of flies at a time. How glad they were to have long tails then!

But Clopper couldn't swish away the flies, because his tail was short. He had to stand in the field and feel them running all over him and often biting him. He couldn't bear it! He scampered here and he scampered there, trying to shake the flies off his back. He reared and he stamped – but as soon as he had scared the flies away, down they came again!

Cluck was very sorry for him. How she wished he had a proper tail. Poor Clopper!

One morning she went to him. 'Clopper. I've thought of a way to help you. You said you'd never need my help, but you do. Listen, will you please lie down in the grass and let me show you what I can do?'

Clopper lay down in surprise. The flies flew down to him as soon as he was still. Then little Cluck hopped up on to his back.

'Keep still, Clopper, keep still!' she clucked. 'I'm going to peck up and eat every fly I see! Keep still!'

Clopper felt Cluck's little feet running up and down his back and she pecked up flies here, there and everywhere! Oh how wonderful! Not one was biting him now, not one was annoying him!

'I've eaten every one,' said Cluck. 'And I believe they're scared of me now. They're not flying down, anyway. I'll just sit myself in the middle of your back, Clopper, and wait till more come – then I'll be after them again.'

And do you know, every single day after that Cluck went to jump on Clopper's back to help him with the flies. Don't you think it was a very, very good idea?

'You see, I was right!' said Cluck. 'Little things *can* help big things!'

Yes, you are right, Cluck. You certainly are a good friend to Clopper! I *wondered* what you were doing up there on his back! Now I know!

Patter's Adventure

Patter's Adventure

IN A hole in a bank at the bottom of Mary's garden lived a mouse family. They were long-tailed field mice, pretty little things, and as playful as could be.

Every day the mother mouse ran off to get food for the family. She knew exactly where to get it. Mary kept two doves in a cage, and she fed them each day, sometimes with grain and sometimes with bread.

The mouse was small enough to creep under the big cage where the doves lived and take a piece of bread. Before the doves could peck her she was out again, running down the garden with the bread. Then the little mouse family would have a lovely feast.

Now, one day Patter, the youngest of the family, wanted an adventure. He had often heard his mother talk of the wonderful place where bread could always be found, and he wanted to see it for himself. So he followed his mother and saw where she went.

But as she came back she saw Patter. She dropped the bread at once and flew at him. 'Patter! You bad, naughty little mouse! How dare you come out alone like this! Don't you know that Bubbles the cat is about?'

Patter had no idea what a cat was. He stared at his mother and his tiny nose went up and down. He curled his long tail round his little body and looked miserable.

'What's a cat?' he said.

'Oh, my baby! Fancy asking what a CAT is!' said his mother. 'You'll know soon enough one day if you run about alone when you're no more than a few days old!'

She took Patter back and gave him such a talking to that he didn't stir out of the nest for days. Then he suddenly felt that he must have an adventure again. And this time, he thought, he would go by himself right up to the doves' cage and find a bit of bread on his own. Then he could eat it all without having to share it with four brothers and sisters.

So off he went, a little tiny thing almost small enough to pop under a thimble!

Now Bubbles the cat had three growing kittens. They were five weeks old and very playful. They rolled about, they climbed out of their basket and they ran unsteadily over the kitchen floor. They often tried to catch their mother's tail.

'It is time you stopped being babies,' said Bubbles one night. 'You must learn what it is to hunt for mice. One day you will have to catch food for yourselves, and I must teach you.'

'What are mice?' asked Ginger, who was the biggest kitten. Bubbles was astonished.

'What! You don't know what mice are! I will catch one and bring it in for you. You shall play with it, catch it for yourselves and eat it. Mice are very tasty.'

So out Bubbles went, the same night that Patter was off on his adventure. She knew that mice went to the doves' cage, because she had smelt them. Perhaps there would be a nice, lively mouse tonight. She would catch him and take him to her kittens!

Patter was running down the garden path to the cage. What a dear little mouse, with his woffly nose and long, thin tail and fine whiskers!

But Bubbles the cat was waiting by the cage. Patter didn't know that. He came to the cage and sniffed. He could smell CAT, but he didn't know what it was, so he wasn't afraid. He could smell bread too, and that made his nose twitch more than ever.

Bubbles smelt him and sat there without moving even a paw. Patter ran nearer. He was just about to squeeze under the cage when he felt a strong paw pounce on him. He gave a loud squeak. 'Eeeeee!'

He wriggled, but he couldn't get away. The paw held him, and he felt sharp claws sticking into him as soon as he moved. He was terribly afraid. Was this CAT?

The paw moved and scraped him away from the cage. Then hot breath came over him and something sniffed him all over. Then, oh tails and whiskers, the mouth opened and Patter went inside! He was in the cat's mouth, surrounded by sharp teeth.

He squeaked again. He was not hurt, because Bubbles hadn't scratched or bitten him. No – she wanted to take him, whole and unhurt, to her three kittens to play with. They could chase him, pounce on him, throw him into the air and then eat him for their supper. She would teach them what Mouse was.

She padded to the kitchen window, still holding Patter in her hot mouth. His tail hung out from between her teeth. He squeaked and squeaked. Bubbles leapt up to the windowsill and dropped down into the kitchen. She purred, and her three kittens ran to her.

She dropped Patter on the floor, and he stared

round at the wondering kittens. 'There,' said Bubbles. 'That is a mouse. Sniff him well. All mice smell the same. Then chase him and see if you can catch him.'

The kittens stared doubtfully at the mouse. Then one put out a paw to him. Patter leapt away and ran into a corner. The kitten ran after him.

Somebody was sitting in the kitchen rocking chair. It was being rocked to and fro, to and fro. Suddenly the rocking stopped, and a voice called out in horror, 'My goodness! There's a mouse running around the kitchen! My goodness!'

Up got the person in the rocking chair and rushed out of the kitchen. She went to find Mary.

'Can you come, quickly?' she panted. 'You keep pet mice, don't you, so you're not afraid of them. There's a mouse in the kitchen! Bubbles brought it in for her kittens, but it's alive and running around. I can't bear it!'

Mary went into the kitchen. She put Bubbles outside and shut the door. The kittens were still staring at the mouse, not feeling very sure about it. Patter was not at all sure about the kittens either. He felt that he would like to play with them – but they were so big!

Mary saw him. 'Oh, what a darling little field mouse!' she said. 'Go away, kittens, don't hurt it.' She bent down to get it, but Patter, seeing such an enormous person suddenly bending over him, darted under a small table. Mary moved the table and put out her hand to catch Patter. He jumped away and ran right into the three kittens. Ginger put out a paw and tried to claw him. He didn't like that. He ran back under the table again.

And there Mary caught him gently in her hand. She closed her fingers round him so that only his little, woffly nose showed, and his tail hung out at the back.

'You're sweet!' she said. 'I'll show you to Mummy. You're too little to be out in the night by yourself. Whatever shall I do with you?'

She took the mouse to her mother. 'Look,' she said, 'a baby field mouse. Isn't he sweet? What shall I do with him? He'll be caught by Bubbles again, or an owl, if I set him free in the darkness outside.'

'Well, dear, put him with your own pet mice,' said her mother. 'He'll be quite happy with the others and much safer than running about by himself.'

'Will he really?' said Mary. 'I never thought of that! I'll put him into my mouse cage now.'

The mouse cage was outside on the verandah. It was too smelly to be in the house. There were three mice there, one black, one brown and one black-and-white. In the cage was a ladder for the mice to climb up and down, a dish of water and plenty of food. At the top of the cage was a shut-in place, full of straw, which was the bedroom of the mice, very warm and cosy.

Mary lifted off the glass top, and slipped Patter inside. He was frightened now. He didn't like his adventure any more. He wanted to get back home to his mother and her nest. But he knew he would never, never find the way. Mary shone a torch into the cage and watched him.

He ran up the ladder and down. What an exciting place he had come to. But he couldn't get out of it. He sniffed here and he sniffed there – but there was no way out at all.

He could smell other mice. Where were they? He ran up a twig that was set there to lead to the bedroom and saw a round hole with straw sticking out. In a flash he was in the hole.

A ball of mice was curled up in a corner. Patter nosed his way to it and it dissolved into three surprised little pet mice. They all sniffed at Patter.

'He's just a baby,' said Frisky.

'Better make room for him,' said Whisky.

'Come along then,' said Nipper, and into the ball of mice crept Patter, happy and pleased. He cuddled in, wrapped his tail round everybody, stuck his nose into his paws and went to sleep.

His mother was upset when he didn't come back. 'The cat's got him,' she said.

Bubbles felt sure her three kittens had eaten him. 'Did he taste nice?' she asked.

The three kittens felt certain that the mouse had escaped down a hole somewhere, but they didn't dare to tell their mother that. They knew they should have caught him – but they had been just a tiny bit afraid of the jumpity mouse. So they said nothing at all.

Patter is still living with Frisky, Whisky and Nipper, and is as happy as the day is long. His nose is still woffly, his tail is longer than ever and his whiskers are finer. Would you like to see him? He is a real live mouse and this is a real true story. He lives in a mouse cage on my verandah, and we feed him every day.

'Eee!' he says and runs up his little wooden ladder to greet us. 'Eeee!' Wouldn't you love a pet mouse like that?

What Fun it Was!

What Fun it Was!

'THERE GOES Long-Ears the donkey!' said Biddy, as she heard the clip-clop of hooves, and she ran to the window. 'Isn't he a dear? It was lucky that the baker could buy him, wasn't it, Mummy, when his old horse couldn't pull his little bread van any more?'

'It *was* lucky,' said Mummy. 'Mr Bunting depends on his van to sell his bread – he couldn't go pushing a cart at his age.'

Mr Bunting was very glad to have Long-Ears. Sunny, his old horse, had kept on as long as ever he could – but one day he simply lay down in his harness and wouldn't go another step!

'You're too old, Sunny!' said his master sadly. 'Well – I'll just keep you as a pet now – you can live in your field and whinny to the children who come by to stroke your velvety nose. But who shall I get to pull my van now?'

Well, the very next day Billy Brown came by with Long-Ears, his little donkey. Long-Ears lived by the sea and gave children rides on the sand, and made a lot of money for Billy Brown – but now Billy was going to live inland, so Long-Ears was to be sold.

He was sold to Mr Bunting, who was delighted with him, for the donkey was patient, strong and clever.

'Do you know,' said Mr Bunting to his wife, after he had had Long-Ears for two weeks, 'do you know, my dear, that little donkey already knows every house I sell bread to? And what's more, he *stops* at each one before I even say "Whoa!". There's brains for you!'

'Long-Ears is a darling,' said his wife. 'And how he does love the children, to be sure! He knocks on the ground with his hoof when one comes by, as if to say,

"Hey – I'm here! Come and stroke me."'

'And they *do* stroke him,' said Mr Bunting. 'And pat him, and give him carrots and apples. Well, my old horse Sunny was the best friend I ever had – but this little donkey is wonderful.'

Yes, the children certainly loved Long-Ears, and saved up titbits for him. Even Fred, who wasn't fond of animals, came out to give him a carrot when the bread van came. As for Biddy, who lived next door to the baker's shop, she loved Long-Ears more than any of the other children, and always watched out for him.

Long-Ears often gave the children rides on his back, when he had been put in the field where the old horse lived, after his day's work. But sometimes he was too tired, and then, when he saw the children coming, he lay down – and they knew that he was too weary to give them a ride, and just petted him instead.

In the holidays Biddy asked Mr Bunting if she could ride with him in his little van to the next village. 'You see, my auntie lives there,' said Biddy, 'but it costs a shilling to go there and back. She's got a new little baby and I want to go and help her as often as I can.'

'Well,' said the baker, 'I can drop you at her house, because I take her bread to her – and pick you up when I'm on my way back, if you like.'

So each day Biddy went off with Mr Bunting and Long-Ears, the envy of all the children in her village. She was dropped at her aunt's house, and picked up again three hours later – but in that time she managed to help her aunt a great deal.

Biddy had a great surprise the first time she went off with the donkey and Mr Bunting. The baker now didn't even bother to say 'Whoa!' when he came to a customer's house – Long-Ears stopped of his own accord – and actually stamped on the ground with his hoof to let the customer know he was there!

'Oh, Mr Bunting – isn't he clever!' said Biddy in astonishment. 'Look – Mrs Lacy has heard him stamping and has come out for her bread!'

'Yes. I hardly bother to get down from my cart now,' said Mr Bunting, laughing. 'Long-Ears knows my customers' houses – and he knows my customers too! They so often give him a titbit!'

So they did. The little donkey had lumps of sugar, carrots, turnips, apples – anything that his customers knew he liked. He blinked his lovely eyes at them, and offered his velvet-grey nose to be rubbed.

'Ah – he's a good donkey, this one of yours,' said Mrs Lacy, patting his neck. 'What would you do without him, Mr Bunting?'

'That I don't know!' said the old baker. 'I'm stiff in my joints, now, Mrs Lacy – and this little fellow saves me getting up and down from my cart, the way he knocks with his hooves to tell my customers I'm here. I could carry a bell of course – but I think Long-Ears likes to tell everyone he's arrived!'

Sometimes Mr Bunting let Biddy drive the little cart for him. She was very pleased then, and felt most important holding the reins and jogging up and down behind Long-Ears as he trotted along on his sturdy little legs. Biddy's mother was pleased too.

'You're getting rosy cheeks, Biddy, going out into the open air every day with Long-Ears,' she said. 'I hope you try and help Mr Bunting too, whenever you can.'

'Oh, yes,' said Biddy. 'Sometimes the customers don't hear the donkey stamping his hoof to tell them we're there – and then I get down with the little bread basket and run to the house myself. I know all the customers on the way to Auntie's and back!'

Now, one day when Biddy watched at the window for the baker to appear with his little donkey and breadcart, no Mr Bunting arrived! She waited and waited, and then ran to the shop next door to find out why they were so late.

Mrs Bunting was there in tears. 'Oh, Biddy, dear!' she said. 'Poor Mr Bunting fell down the stairs this morning, and hurt his back – and there he is in bed, groaning away, and me waiting and waiting for the doctor to come. And what's to happen to the bread that was baked last night I *don't* know!'

'Oh, dear!' said Biddy. 'Poor Mr Bunting! And what about his customers, Mrs Bunting? They'll have no bread today.'

'I know, I know,' said the baker's wife. 'But what am I to *do*? I'd take the cart out myself, but I must wait for the doctor.'

Then Biddy had a marvellous idea – and she clutched at Mrs Bunting's arm.

'Mrs Bunting – *I* know!' she said. 'Let *me* take the cart! Mr Bunting often lets me drive it – and Long-Ears and I know all the houses where he leaves bread. We do, really!'

'Bless you, child!' said Mrs Bunting. 'But you only know the customers on the way to your aunt's house and back – you don't know them *all*!'

'But *Long-Ears* would know their houses, and stop there, and stamp with his hoof just as he does at every customer's house,' said Biddy. 'I'm sure he would. Mr Bunting has been so kind to take me every day to my auntie's and back, Mrs Bunting – let me do this for him. My mother always says you should return kindness whenever a chance comes.'

'Well, my dear – I don't know what to say,' said Mrs Bunting. 'You'd better go and ask your mother what *she* thinks – and if she says yes, well – I don't see why you shouldn't try. Can you go and get Long-Ears and put him in the cart, do you think?'

'Oh *yes*!' said Biddy, her eyes shining, and she sped off to ask her mother. Oh, if only she could do this! She wasn't very clever at school, and she was slow at games – but here was something she could do better than anyone else now that the baker was ill! Oh, if *only* her mother would say yes!

Her mother listened as Biddy poured out her tale. Then she smiled and nodded her head. 'You're a sensible little girl,' she said. 'I don't see why you shouldn't try to help. Driving a donkey as clever as Long-Ears won't be hard work, and I know you'll let him go at his own pace.'

'Oh, I will, I will!' said Biddy, and gave her mother a sudden hug. 'Mummy, you're a darling to say "yes". I'm off to get Long-Ears now.'

Off she went, and Long-Ears, waiting patiently by the field-gate, wondering why his master was so late, was very pleased to see his friend Biddy. She led him to the cart, talking to him all the time, telling him everything. He listened gravely, his long ears straight up, nodding his head every now and then.

They set off together proudly, Long-Ears pulling the little cart as usual, trotting along quickly. Biddy's mother watched them from the window, feeling proud of her daughter.

'She's kind, she's trustworthy and she's sensible,' said Biddy's mother to herself. 'And what more could I want in a child? How surprised her aunt will be to see her in charge of the donkey and cart today!'

Long-Ears seemed pleased that Biddy was driving him. He was as clever as ever, stopping at each customer's door and stamping with his hoof. Out came the customers – and dear me, *how* astonished they were to see Biddy all alone in the cart! She handed them their bread and told them the news. Then off she went again, Long-Ears watching out for the next customer's house.

It was very easy for Biddy all the way to her aunt's house, for she knew as well as Long-Ears did which house to stop at – but when she went off to another village, she had to depend on the little donkey to stop at the right places.

He did, of course. Here was Cherry Cottage – first stop! Stamp, stamp! – that was the donkey's hoof – and out ran Miss Johnson, surprised not to see Mr Bunting, but instead a little girl she didn't know! 'One loaf, please!' she called, and Biddy handed it down.

Biddy had the baker's account book with her, with the names of all the customers in it and the bread they bought. Biddy carefully jotted down the amount of bread beside the names each time, but she did not need to take any money, because the customers paid only on Saturdays. What with driving the cart, handing out the bread and writing in the little book, Biddy felt busier and happier than she had ever felt in her life before!

'I couldn't do without you in these villages you know, Long-Ears,' she said. 'I simply wouldn't know where to stop – but you *always* know. You must be the cleverest donkey in the world – and the nicest.'

Then Long-Ears stopped at a small white house and stamped. Nobody came out. So Biddy took the little bread basket and ran in at the gate. An old lady was out in the back garden, watering her flowers, and she hadn't heard Long-Ears stamping.

'Dear me – so *you're* the baker today, are you?' she said. 'I'll have one loaf please – and would you like to have a piece of my fruit cake? I made it yesterday and I'm longing to share a piece with someone.'

So Biddy sat down with her and ate fruit cake and drank lemonade, telling the old lady all about poor

Mr Bunting, and how she was helping him.

'Well, well – he's lucky to have a child like you next door!' said the old lady. 'Now – surely I hear Long-Ears stamping? I must get him a carrot.'

So the donkey had a feast too and gave the old lady a loud hee-haw of thanks before he trotted off again with Biddy and the cart.

He had plenty of titbits that day – and so did Biddy! In fact she had never had such a wonderful day in her life. She felt very proud as she drove down her own village street, four hours later, nearly all the bread sold, and every loaf entered properly against the name of each customer.

'Look! Look at Biddy driving Long-Ears all by herself!' shouted the children. 'Hey, Biddy – are you the baker today?'

'Yes, I am!' shouted back Biddy. 'I've done the whole round – and Long-Ears and I never once made a mistake!'

She went in to see Mrs Bunting, and gave her the

baker's book. The baker's wife gave her a hug, really delighted that she had done so well.

'Mr Bunting has to rest for five days,' she said. 'Then he'll be all right again. Well, Biddy dear, would you like to take Long-Ears round with the cart till Mr Bunting is better? His nephew is coming over each night to bake the bread – so it will be ready to take round each morning as usual.'

'Oh – I'd LOVE to!' said Biddy delighted. 'I can't tell you what fun it was, Mrs Bunting – but, of course, I couldn't have done it without Long-Ears – he knew where every customer lived, and stamped each time to let them know we were there.'

'He's a good donkey – and you're a good girl!' said Mrs Bunting. 'Your mother should be proud of you, and your father too. Now you go upstairs and tell Mr Bunting all about your day.'

Biddy was very happy. To think she could drive Long-Ears round the villages for five days more! *how* all the children would stare!

So there she is, clicking to the little donkey each morning, as they start off together, Long-Ears as happy as she is. She knows every customer now – but what she *doesn't* know is that Mr Bunting is going to give her a lovely little brooch at the end of the week – and on it is a little donkey, *exactly* like – Long-Ears!

Won't she be pleased?

The Goose that Made a Hurricane

The Goose that Made a Hurricane

ONCE UPON a time there was a big grey goose. She had very large wings and when she stood on her toes and flapped them, she made quite a wind.

One day she went to a little hillock and, standing on the top, she flapped her wings very hard indeed. No sooner had she finished than a wind began to blow from the west. It almost blew the grey goose off the hillock and she looked round her in surprise.

'Good gracious!' she said. 'Look what a wind I've started! I only just flapped my wings a few times, and I have made this great wind! How powerful I am! I must go and tell Porker the pig.'

So off she waddled. Soon she came to the sty where Porker the pig lived. Bits of straw were flying all about and Porker was standing with his back to the wind, for he did not like it.

'I've some news for you, Porker,' said the grey goose. 'Do you know, I just stood up on the little hillock and flapped my wings a few times, and that started this big wind blowing!'

'What a strange thing!' said Porker, staring at the grey goose with his little round eyes. 'Shall we go and tell Gobble the turkey?'

'Yes, let's,' said the goose proudly. So they went across the farmyard to where Gobble the turkey was sheltering from the wind which now had almost become a gale.

'We've some news for you, Gobble,' said Porker the pig. 'Do you know, the grey goose just stood up on the little hillock to flap her wings a few times, and that started this big wind blowing!'

'What a curious thing!' said Gobble, staring at the

grey goose in surprise. 'Shall we go and tell Neddy the donkey?'

'Yes, let's,' said the grey goose and the pig. So they went across to the field where Neddy the donkey was standing beneath a tree, trying to get away from the great wind.

'We've some news for you, Neddy,' said Gobble the turkey. 'Do you know, the grey goose just stood up on the little hillock to flap her wings a few times, and that started this big wind blowing!'

'What a wonderful thing!' said Neddy, staring at the grey goose in astonishment. 'Shall we go and tell Frisky the lamb?'

'Yes, let's,' said the grey goose, the pig and the turkey. So they hurried to the other end of the field where Frisky the lamb stood by himself, very much frightened of the big wind that was almost blowing his long tail off.

'We've some news for you, Frisky,' said Neddy the donkey. 'Do you know, the grey goose just stood up on the little hillock to flap her wings a few times, and that started this big wind blowing!'

'What a funny thing!' said Frisky, staring at the grey goose with startled eyes. 'Shall we go and tell Trotter the horse?'

'Yes, let's,' said the grey goose, the pig, the turkey and the donkey. So they hurried to the farmyard and went to the shed where Trotter stood, listening to the big gale that blew all around.

'We've some news for you, Trotter,' said Frisky the lamb. 'Do you know, the grey goose just stood up on the little hillock to flap her wing a few times, and that started this big wind blowing!'

'What a marvellous thing!' said old Trotter the horse. 'If she can do things like that, you had better make her queen of the farmyard!'

So they made the grey goose queen, and she was very proud indeed.

The wind went on blowing and blowing. It got stronger and stronger, it became a gale, and then it turned into a hurricane and blew roofs and tiles and chimneys off! Everyone was frightened, and all the farmyard folk went to hide. Only the grey goose was pleased, for she was queen, and she was proud to think she had caused such a terrible gale.

After a time, Rover the yard dog came trotting into the yard, his ears blown flat back by the wind. He looked very cross indeed.

'What's the matter?' Porker asked.

'Quite enough!' growled Rover. 'I was eating the finest, juiciest bone I'd had for months when this great gale blew up from nowhere and took my bone along with it!'

'Oh, this gale didn't spring up from nowhere,' said Porker the pig. 'Haven't you heard the news? We've made the grey goose queen of the farmyard because she was clever enough to start this hurricane by just flapping her wings a few times! Isn't she wonderful!'

'No, she isn't,' said Rover, in a temper. 'The horrid gale has blown away my bone. And what nonsense to say a goose could start a wind! Can she stop it, Porker, do you know? If she can start it, she can stop it, and perhaps I can find my bone again.'

'Oh, I'm sure she can stop it,' said the pig. 'Come and ask her!'

So they went to ask the grey goose to stop the hurricane.

'It's your gale,' said Rover, 'so just stop it, grey goose. It's taken away my best bone.'

The grey goose stood up on her toes, opened her beak and shouted 'Stop!' to the gale. But it didn't take any notice at all. It just went on blowing and roaring and racing.

'I don't believe you started this wind,' said the dog. 'You're only a silly, ordinary goose, so how could you? You think too much of yourself, that's what it is! Hurry up and stop it!'

'I *did* start the gale!' said the grey goose. 'Look, I just stood up like this and opened out my wings like this – Oh! Oh! Oh!' And well might the poor grey goose cry 'Oh, oh, oh!' for the wind took hold of her big wings and lifted her right up into the air. Off she went with the gale, and all the farmyard stared in astonishment and wonder.

'That's what comes of meddling with winds and things like that,' said Rover. 'My advice to you all is to go to your sheds and hide there until this dreadful hurricane is over!'

Off they all went, hurry-scurry, the pig and the turkey, the donkey and the lamb, the horse and the dog. But as for the grey goose, no one has ever heard what became of her, for she was never seen again.

Acknowledgements

All efforts have been made to seek necessary permissions.

The stories in this publication first appeared in the following publications:

'The Dog with the Very Long Tail' first appeared in *Sunny Stories for Little Folks*, No. 105, 1930.

'The Gentle Scarecrow' first appeared in *Sunny Stories for Little Folks*, No. 235, 1936.

'Whiskers and Balloon-Face' first appeared as 'Tinker and Balloon-Face' in *Enid Blyton's Sunny Stories*, No. 335, 1944.

'The New Little Calves' first appeared in *Down at the Farm with Enid Blyton*, published by Sampson Low in 1951.

'The Careless Hedgehogs' first appeared in *Merry Moments*, No. 182, 1922.

'Micky's Present' first appeared in *Enid Blyton's Sunny Stories*, No. 148, 1939.

'Bushy's Secret' first appeared in *The Teacher's Treasury*, Vol. 1, published by The Home Library Book Company in 1926.

'The Tale of Flop and Whiskers' first appeared in *Sunny Stories for Little Folks*, No. 193, 1934.

'Where Was Baby Pam?' first appeared in *Sunny Stories for Little Folks*, No. 162, 1933.

'The Runaway Mouse' first appeared in *Sunny Stories for Little Folks*, No. 154, 1932.

'How John Got His Ducklings' first appeared in *Sunny Stories for Little Folks*, No. 183, 1934.

'The Remarkable Tail' first appeared in *The Dancing Doll and other stories*, published by Parragon in 1997.

'Goldie, the Cat Who Said Thank You' first appeared in *The Teacher's Treasury*, Vol. 1, published by The Home Library Book Company in 1926.

'Tie a Knot in His Tail' first appeared in *Enid Blyton's Magazine*, No. 23, Vol. 2, 1954.

'It Takes All Sorts to Make a World' first appeared in *Sunday Mail*, No. 1899, 1945.

'A Shock for Mr Meanie' first appeared as 'A Shock for Mr. Meanie' in *Enid Blyton's Sunny Stories*, No. 397, 1947.

'A Ride on a Horse' first appeared in *Down at the Farm with Enid Blyton*, pubished by Sampson Low in 1951.

'Where's the Kitten?' first appeared in *Enid Blyton's Magazine*, No. 21, 1956.

'The Poor Pink Pig' first appeared in *Sunny Stories for Little Folks*, No. 178, 1933.

'Here You Are, Squirrel!' first appeared in *Enid Blyton's Magazine*, No. 2, Vol. 3, 1955.

'The Bowl of Bread and Milk' first appeared in *Sunny Stories for Little Folks*, No. 96, 1930.

'Cosy's Good Turn' first appeared in *Daily Mail Annual for Boys and Girls*, 1945.

'The Rabbit's Whiskers' first appeared in *Sunny Stories for Little Folks*, No. 148, 1932.

'Who-Who-Who-Who?' first appeared in *The Enid Blyton Nature Readers*, No. 15, published by Macmillan in 1945.

'He Was Clever After All!' first appeared as 'He Was Clever, After All!' in *Enid Blyton's Sunny Stories*, No. 393, 1946.

'The Three Pixies and the Cats' first appeared as 'The Three Golliwogs and the Cats' in *Enid Blyton's Sunny Stories*, No. 280, 1942.

'The Tale of Cluck and Clopper' first appeared in *Enid Blyton's Magazine*, No. 12, Vol. 2, 1954.

'Patter's Adventure' first appeared in *Enid Blyton's Sunny Stories*, No. 380, 1946.

'What Fun it Was!' first appeared in *Enid Blyton's Magazine*, No. 7, Vol. 4, 1956.

'The Goose that Made a Hurricane' first appeared in *Sunny Stories for Little Folks*, No. 90, 1930.

Also available:

Delve into the world of our furry and feathered friends with these short stories by the world's best-loved storyteller!

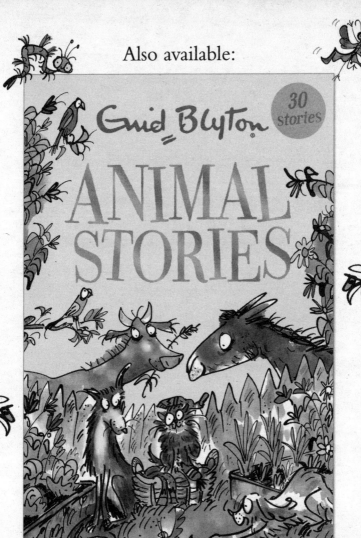

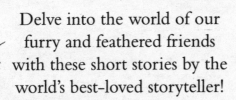

Gather up your furry friends for these short stories by the world's best-loved storyteller.

Enid Blyton®

THE FAMOUS FIVE

Join the Adventure!

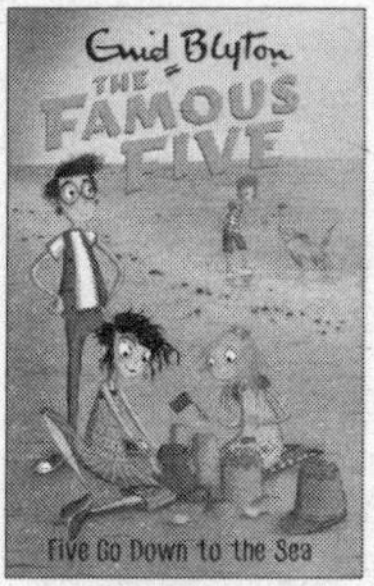

Have you read them all?

Also available

an irrisistible new story by bestselling author Jacqueline Wilson.

Mia, Milo and Birdy are on a countryside holiday when they discover the Enchanted Wood. Join their adventures up the Magic Faraway Tree with Moonface, Saucepan Man and Silky the fairy.

Enid Blyton®

is one of the most popular children's authors of all time. Her books have sold over 500 million copies and have been translated into other languages more often than any other children's author.

Enid Blyton adored writing for children. She wrote over 700 books and about 2,000 short stories. *The Famous Five* books, now 80 years old, are her most popular. She is also the author of other favourites including *The Secret Seven*, *The Magic Faraway Tree* and *Malory Towers*.

Born in London in 1897, Enid lived much of her life in Buckinghamshire and loved dogs, gardening and the countryside. She was very knowledgeable about trees, flowers, birds and animals. Dorset – where some of the Famous Five's adventures are set – was a favourite place of hers too.

Enid Blyton's stories are read and loved by millions of children (and grown-ups) all over the world. Visit enidblyton.co.uk to discover more.

Illustration by Laura Ellen Anderson.